Fate

CURSE OF FATE

BOOK TWO

SAMANTHA BARRETT

For my husband.

*To my knight in shining armor, you are my everything.
I love you today, tomorrow and forever.
Thank you for being you and loving me completely.
"Forever with you would never be long enough."*

"You have to do the spell; the boys will know what spell to procure. Trust in yourself, you can do this."

"How can you be so sure?"

"Because you are stronger than you know. He will need to play his part—you must do this spell."

I drifted out of my daydream and sighed. Yeah, I wasn't just dreaming while sleeping now.

I sit in my room, gazing out the window, not really seeing anything. The doubts of what I am supposed to do are creeping in. Kai's gone. He's actually fucking gone.

I feel the tears starting to build again. Taking a steadying breath, I push my emotions back down. I can't give into my grief when there is a chance the tears will be wasted. I've spent the past three days in this room, planning and plotting.

Losing Kai was a hard pill to swallow; I didn't even get the chance to really get to know him. I shake myself out of my thoughts. I need to get my head back in the game and stick to the plan if I want vengeance for Kai.

I take my first shower in who knows how long and slip on the clothes Aurora brought me. They fit like a glove, but even if they didn't, beggars can't be choosers. I quickly brush my hair and teeth and, taking a deep breath, I brave leaving my room.

I try to make my way to the mess hall, where I assume everyone will be. I haven't seen Dom, Jax, or Nico since I awoke after losing Kai. I'm anxious to see them.

Guilt has me stumbling. I lied; I'm not anxious to see *them*, I'm anxious to see *him*. When I found out that Kai was real, I knew there was a slim chance Nico was too. Kai may be dead, and here I am being a worthless piece of shit, pining after his best friend. Now that I know the truth, I shouldn't feel guilt for my feelings toward Nico, but I do.

I refuse to let my mind wonder anymore. I need to find the guys and make a plan. After turning down many different hallways and then retracing my steps because I went the wrong way, I finally got to the mess hall. I can hear muffled sounds coming from inside the hall. I know people are going to stare, but before I can talk myself out of it, I push the doors open and enter.

As soon as I walk in, all conversation stops. I can feel so many pairs of eyes on me. I hold my head high and make my way to the food station. It takes all of ten seconds before both my cousins are beside me.

"Squirt, you don't have to be here." I count to three in my head and then address Alex.

"I know, but sitting in that room and feeling sorry for myself isn't going to help anyone, is it?" I don't mean to sound bitchy, but I need to keep up my act that I'm grieving. I need to make sure to keep my answers vague in front of Jackson or he will know I'm lying.

"If you need to be angry, then do that. But don't let any of these assholes see you hurting. We're here with you every step of the way, cousin." Chase's words helped ease some of the tension in my body. I kept my head held high, grabbed my food, and followed the boys back to their table.

I feel it the instant his eyes lock on me; I feel a sizzle zapping down my spine. I avoid eye contact and take the seat between Alex and Chase. No one speaks for a long moment. I push the food around my plate, not having much of an appetite due to someone's gaze burning holes in me.

"It's good to see you, Ryan." I don't need to look up to know its Aurora that spoke. Again, I count to three in my head before lifting my eyes to hers. The look on her face is nearly my undoing— so much pity shines within them. "We're all here for you."

How am I supposed to reply to that? I know Jax and Dom are waiting for me to acknowledge their presence, but in order for me to do that, I would have to see *him*. And as if sensing my inner struggle, *he* speaks.

"I know you are hurting." God, the sound of his voice is making me feel things. Things I don't want to feel right now.

"We need to speak with you, privately." I don't voice a reply or lift my head. I simply nod. After a minute or so, conversation around the table continues, and I zone out, lost in my own thoughts.

"Ryan, did you hear me?" I turn toward Chase, staring into his sky-blue eyes. I shake my head.

"I just said, if you are done eating, we should go to Jackson's office and *talk*." I nod and stand, following the group to Jackson's office. Once we enter the room, I move to the couch and sit down on the far end, so I don't have to be seated between anyone. I don't make eye contact or speak to the others as they all find their own seats. Someone clears their throat; I look up and quickly scan the room. Jax, Dom, and Aurora share a couch. Chase is beside me and Alex beside him. *He* sits in the lone chair in the middle, and I don't make eye contact. I pretend he isn't even there. It's easier if I pretend my feelings for him don't exist. My heart has no place in this war, plus I can't trust him. He has no idea I know about his lies and secrets. It's crazy that after everything he has done, I still want him to hold me. I want him to tell me we'll be okay and we can make this work. I quickly shake my thoughts away, and ask the pertinent question.

"So, what do you all want to talk about? Please don't treat me like I am made of glass." I'm quite proud of myself; my voice is strong and steady.

"We need to make a plan to move forward with unlocking your powers" There it is, the reason why everyone is so tense. Did they think I would back out?

"I agree, when should we start?" Jax looked shocked. I agreed with him so easily. They were all giving me strange looks now, almost as if they expected me to have a tantrum and let a world die. I would never do something like that; I gave my word and I will not go back on that promise.

"Ahhhh... Okay, I thought that we were going to have to convince you, Squirt. I guess the next question is what do we do now?" Oh, Alex, if only you knew the full story.

"Before all this happens, we need to make sure that you are ready for what comes next, love." I wish they would all stop beating around the bush.

"Just say it, Dom." I made sure to keep my face blank of all emotion. I couldn't afford for them to see beyond the mask I was wearing.

"Okay, Love, are you ready to take your sister down?" Dom asks, never breaking eye contact. Looking into his violet eyes was almost hypnotizing.

"Yes, I will do whatever needs to be done to ensure the safety of the fae realm. My sister will pay for what she has done." I meant every single word; I waited for the sting to come, knowing that I had just vowed to destroy my sister, but I felt nothing. I was numb. Stevie made her choice, and I have made mine.

"Tonight, we will need to head toward the northern border. It's far enough away from the pack and humans." Jackson's concern for his pack and the humans in the area was touching but unnecessary. My powers wouldn't be unlocked tonight—not that *he* would tell the group why that is. I needed to keep up my act by playing along like I didn't know the truth.

"What happens if you can't control the blast, Dom?" I asked, and judging by the looks on the others faces, they were all wondering the same thing.

"I will try my best. I have never had to contain something like this before." I appreciated his honesty. "If we are far enough away from the pack and humans we should be fine." Dom then turned to *him* and asked, "You would have more of an idea than any of us, brother—what do you think?"

"I think what Jax has planned is the best option. I don't know exactly what the blast radius will be." His voice was like music, a beautiful tune that you didn't want to stop. "I think we should start tonight." Before he could continue to torment me with his song, Aurora started to shake and her eyes went white. Dom and Jax quickly jumped from their seats, followed by Alex and Chase. Alex went to reach for her but Jax slapped his hand away.

"You cannot touch her! If you do, it could cause her harm."

After what felt like hours but was only minutes, Aurora finally stopped shaking, and her eyes returned to their normal pale blue color. No one spoke. We were giving her time to sort her thoughts and gather herself. Jax made his way over to his desk and grabbed the bottle of water that was sitting there; he returned and handed it to Aurora, who thanked him and took two big sips.

"I'm sorry, I didn't mean to scare you all. I think you should all sit down. I didn't see anything good, I'm afraid" Aurora gave me a strange look. I was starting to panic now—what if she saw and knew the whole truth? I couldn't risk them finding out now, not yet. I just hoped that she only saw what *he* wasn't telling the group.

The four guys take their seats, all eyes turn to Aurora, waiting. Shaking her head and taking a few calming breaths, she spoke, looking me dead in the eyes. *Oh God, please.*

"Ryan, you can't unlock your powers. I had a vision, obviously. If you attempt to unlock your powers, you will die, and—" Nico cuts her off before she can finish.

"That can't be! I put the lock on her powers"

"Yes, but what you don't know is Ryan's father changed the key to unlocking her gifts. Ralph only needed your help to lock her fae power down. He couldn't risk you wanting to claim the greatest weapon."

"Okay, so Ryan's father changed this *key*... What happens now? How does she unlock her powers?" Oh, Alex, you are going to be so pissed.

"She will need to merge with her intended."

"What the hell does that mean, Rora?" *Rora?* Since fucking when did Chase give her a nickname? I didn't realize they were besties now. Aurora turns her gaze back to me.

"Remember I told you that you would need to marry?" I give her a stiff nod. "You need to marry so your power can merge through you both and not kill you. I know this isn't what you want to hear but..." I cut in, not wanting to sit here and hear her continue to beat around the fucking bush. Steeling my spine, I turn to face Nico and look directly into his eyes for the first time.

"So, when should we get hitched, future husband?"

CHAPTER 2

Nico

What the hell!

How did she know? She's looking at me with so much anger and mistrust. Did Aurora betray me? Everyone is staring at me, and Jackson looks like he is two seconds away from wringing my neck.

"Well? Are you going to answer me or sit there like a fish out of water?" I gulp, I know Jax heard. I think that's the only reason why the hateful look he is aiming at me is starting to fade from his face.

"I...I...how?" I sound like a blubbering idiot, but she has me stumped. She is loving every minute of this, judging by the smirk on her beautiful face.

"Oh, you mean how did I know you and Aurora are both lying assholes? That's easy, I have a secret power for sniffing out bullshit!" There is so much venom lacing each of her words. Aurora has a hand clamped across her mouth in shock. So she didn't rat me out after all...who did, then?

"What secret power? And what the fuck is going on here, Squirt?" Her cousin is clearly pissed that he was in the dark about the little bomb she just dropped. She pulls her hateful stare from me to face Alex.

"I can't tell you, Alex. All you need to know is when Aurora dropped the bomb about me needing to marry, she meant I had to marry *him*." Alex spins his stare from Ryan to Aurora, an unmistakable look of hurt on his face. Ah, the young warlock has a crush.

"Why would you hide this from us? You have had so many chances to come clean. I think you need to start telling everyone the fucking truth!" Alex is pissed. Aurora is shaking; she hates having to lie. She looks my way, waiting for me to give her confirmation that she could tell the others the truth. It was time they all knew. I give Aurora a small nod.

"Okay, let's start from the beginning then. I wasn't lying when I told you that in order for your powers to become unstoppable that you needed to marry. What I didn't know at the time was that your father added a failsafe to be sure no one could do this without your consent." I didn't like where she was going with this. "You cannot be forced to marry; you must *choose* to marry. You must also *want* to unlock your powers"

If there was more to her explanation, we wouldn't know, because as soon as she said the last part, everyone was shouting and talking over each other. It was fucking madness. All at once the conversations stopped, and everyone turned to Ryan. She was glowing, staring my way, pointing an accusing finger.

"You bastard! You planned this, didn't you? You knew the whole fucking time that I would need to choose you. That's why you never fought Kai; you always knew I had to *choose* you in the fucking end." Before I could even respond I was blasted from the chair and sent sailing through the air. I hit the back wall with a thud and dropped to the ground. Fuck, that hurt like a bitch. Groaning, I used the wall as support to get me to my feet. My legs were shaky and protesting. That blast she sent had a punch packed within it; she intended to hurt me.

Once on my feet, I pushed away from the wall and turned to face the others. All of them have a look of shock on their faces, except Jackson. He looks smug. Ryan is still glaring daggers my way.

"If you really thought that, you wouldn't be this angry. I never fought my brother because I thought you might be better off with him than with me. I swear to you, love, I didn't know your father altered the key. As far as I knew, all I had to do was remove the bonds I had on your power. I knew you had to marry, but I didn't find out you had to marry *me* until recently." I was praying she could hear the truth in my words; I would never lie to her about this. Did I want her to choose me? Of course, but not like this, where she didn't have a choice.

"Nico is telling the truth. The vision I had showed me what your father had done, afterward." How the hell did Aurora keep getting visions and messages from Ralph Knox? Also, why the hell was she not telling anyone? Something more was going on with this seer, and I am going to find out what it is.

"What exactly did my father do? Don't fucking lie to me, Aurora." Aurora flinched at Ryan's tone, and I don't think she was the only one.

"He added a spell to Nico's. If Nico lifts his bonds, your fae power will surge through you and burn you on the way out. No blast radius, just your death. I have no idea how Ralph knew you would meet a seer, especially one who can see the past and the future."

Jackson butted in before Aurora could finish.

"She cannot marry him, she is my mate!"

I was about to answer, but Ryan beat me to it. She made her way over to Jax and knelt down in front of him. Placing both her hands on top of his, she looked directly into his eyes.

"Jax, I am not your mate." Jackson sucked in a big gulp of air. "You were tricked into thinking that I was. I'm sorry, but I am not your mate." No one spoke for a long while, tension-filled moment. How the hell did she know that? Dom looked from me to Ryan, then to Jax and Aurora. I saw the moment when Dom figured it out; he knew what we did. Dom glared at me.

"You have pulled some shit in the past, brother, but this takes the fucking cake. Why? Why would you do this to him?"

"Because it served his endgame! He knew what he was doing. Didn't you, Nico? You like to fuck with people's lives, lie to them, then tell them you love them." I couldn't look Ryan in the eyes; her words hurt more than she would ever know. "Answer the fucking question, Nico. Why did you do this to him?" I didn't get a chance to answer, Aurora answered instead.

"Because I asked Nico to cast the spell."

"What fucking spell?" Jax was pissed, and it was all my fault. I never meant to hurt him; it wasn't supposed to go this far.

"To conceal who your true mate is. I asked him to find a way to deceive you and throw you off the scent of your mate." Jax snapped his head in Aurora's direction, the tension was rolling off him in waves.

"Why?" That one word sent dread sliding down my spine.

"Because I was trying to stop the future from happening."

"What the fuck does that mean, Aurora?"

"It means *I* am your mate, Jackson. I don't want to be, though; that's why I asked Nico to help me. He never meant for you to think Ryan was your mate, your attraction to her led you to think she was your mate, I think." Jackson fell back into the couch, like someone had slapped him. Ryan clutched his hands tighter, offering her silent support to her friend.

"You don't want to be my mate? So you decided to trick me, hurt me, and lie to me. Why not just come clean and tell me the truth, Aurora? Why go behind my back and ask that piece of shit—who is supposed to be my brother—for help?" Aurora looked to me for assistance. I knew that it was time for the whole truth to come out. Clearing my throat, I addressed the whole room.

"Aurora came to me and told me about the situation, and I offered to help. The only reason she lied to everyone is because—"

Aurora interrupted. "If you mate with me, Jackson, you will die. I have seen it, and I want to change your future. I have never interfered with my visions before, but I cannot let you die. I told you all once that I would have to marry someone I didn't love; that someone is you, Jackson." I was proud of her for voicing her deepest secret.

"Wait! Jackson is not fucking dying." I could hear the alarm in Dom's voice. He wouldn't lose another brother.

"If he mates with me, he will. I am born from wolves, and yet I cannot shift; I am a seer. Jackson is alpha to all wolf packs, and our offspring would be hybrids. No one will understand, and the packs will turn on Jackson. The pack is in uproar now, as they believe he has mated with a witch. No wolf has ever mated outside of their race before." Chase, Alex and Ryan were deathly silent; Dom was trying to remain calm. Jax, on the other hand, just looked defeated.

CHAPTER 3

Ryan

I can see the look of heartbreak on Jax's face. He's devastated. He thought I was his mate, only to be told that I wasn't, and to make matters worse, his true mate has rejected him. Jackson's expression changes from heartbreak to betrayal. The woman he trusted so much has lied to him and broken his trust in the worst way possible. No one says a word as we wait for Jax to process the information and all its ramifications.

"I think we should forget about this conversation and move on to figuring out how to help Ryan." I was grateful for the subject change, but at the same time I would love to slap Chase for bringing the attention back to me. So, I did what any grown-ass woman would do in that moment—I stalled.

"I think we should all take a break and reconvene tonight. It seems like we could all use some time to ourselves." Everyone quickly agreed and started shuffling out of the office.

Jackson stayed behind, claiming he had pack business that he needed to attend to. Honestly, I think he just didn't want to face anyone right now. I couldn't blame him for that. I made my way back to the bedroom I was currently occupying. Once inside the room, I shucked off my shoes and headed for the bed.

I needed to close my eyes and let my mind go blank. Just as I was starting to relax, and my mind finally stopped running away with all different kinds of possibilities, someone knocked on the damn door. Fuck me! I was so damn close! Not bothering to sit up, I called out.

"Come in." I heard heavy footsteps and then the door clicked shut. Peeling one eye open, I turned slightly to see who had entered and groaned.

"What do you want, Nico?" I didn't want to be alone with him; it wasn't a good idea for either of us.

"I just want to explain and talk to you. I know I don't have the right to ask this, but I had my reasons for skirting around the truth." Oh, this should be good. Apparently fae can't lie but Nico manages to navigate around this rule perfectly.

"You have five minutes." I was already doing the countdown in my head. He made his way over to the single chair near the window, resting his forearms on his knees. The T-shirt he was wearing was stretched to its limits. Fuck, he was huge, and he could pull off a plain white tee and jeans like no other.

His beautiful, jet black hair was slightly longer now. I was glad he wasn't looking at me, his deep violet eyes are like a vortex, they would suck me in and I would crumble.

That sounds so cliché, I know, but Nico had a hold over me; it was like there was a string constantly pulling me toward him. It was so hard to fight it but I had to, he lied to me and hurt me. Now that my mind was finally clear after years, I felt so much more for him than I should. I wanted to hate him but I couldn't.

"I'm sorry I deceived you." He was off to an okay start. "I never should have, but I was only trying to protect you from getting hurt. I had no idea your father put a failsafe spell on you after I locked your powers. I swear." I could hear the truth in his voice, but he wasn't getting off the hook that easy.

"You knew I had to marry you, though?"

"I only found out a few days before you came to my realm."

"Aurora came to Farrarie?" I saw him tense and then take a few deep breaths. I could tell he didn't want to tell me, but he knew if he didn't I would kick him out.

"I went to Aurora, she and I would meet every month to re-do the spell masking her scent. She told me then." What the actual fuck! He and Aurora had been doing this for months? Poor Jackson.

"Why let Jackson think I was his mate, then?"

"It was never meant to end like this. Aurora just needed some time to figure out another way. She wanted to find a powerful witch and see if they could break the mate bond. She knew it would be a challenge; if she and Jackson mate, she will need to carry an heir, and if she does that, she will no longer be a seer. She wants to keep her gifts so she can monitor Jackson's future." Oh, I didn't know that part.

"She said in Jackson's office not long ago that she didn't love the man she was supposed to marry. But what I saw today was the total opposite."

"You're right, she is in love with Jax, that is why she will not mate with him." Go figure, how bloody confusing.

"What makes her think she has to carry an heir? They can adopt." As soon as I finished speaking, I wanted to slap myself. Of course they couldn't adopt. Jackson was a fucking shifter.

"Forget I said that, I had a brain fart." Nico started laughing, and I sat up to glare at him, but paused. He looked so carefree and relaxed. I was taken aback; he never looked like this, except when we were having sex, in my dreams. Just thinking about that made me blush. I looked to Nico, who stopped laughing immediately, and the way he was looking at me made me think he knew exactly where my mind had drifted.

Clearing his throat he asked, "What is a brain fart, love?" Screw my life, he had to bring that up, didn't he?

"It's where your mind goes blank for a second, okay? Let's never mention me saying that again, please." He gave a little chuckle, then his face went serious again. I turned so I wasn't looking directly at him; his beauty always distracted me.

"Aurora keeps the pack safe. She sees what will happen and when. If she were to mate and become pregnant, she would lose that advantage. She loves Jackson enough to never endanger his safety." My heart kind of hurt for her. She would give up Jax for him to live.

"That is the stupidest thing I have ever heard; Jax wouldn't care. I am so annoyed that you both felt the need to lie and then cast a spell to trick him. He was just starting to forgive you, Nico. Now you have gone and fucked that up again." I saw him flinch at my words, but I don't feel sorry for him. He knows how I feel about lies, and yet he still felt the need to do it, again. I know this wasn't all his fault, but he could have come clean at any time. Poor Jackson.

"The spell was never meant to make him think you were his mate. I think his initial attraction to you made him feel all of the things he would feel toward a mate. I will not get involved anymore, I swear— she is going through enough as it is."

He's not wrong. Her brother is a fucking rat and a traitor. Tyler was Jackson's right-hand man, his beta. We only found out that he betrayed us when Kai told us the truth.

Kai. Oh, my heart hurt just thinking about him. Kai was so beautiful. He had the most striking gray-blue eyes that I swear could see into your soul. He had light blond hair that you wanted to run your fingers through. I loved Kai, or I thought I did, but he was never mine to love. My twin sister killed him, with the help of Randall Cane, king of all vampires.

I learned recently that my heart needed to stay out of all this mess. My sister would use my love against me and hurt those I cared about. Shaking myself out of my thoughts, I ask Nico the question that has been bugging me for days.

"Did you know that Kai tried to make me fall in love with him so that I would never choose you?" I heard him gasp; clearly he didn't know. I was hurt by Kai's deceit. His betrayal burned like acid. I thought I loved him, and that makes me more angry. I understand why he did it, though. I can never tell the others how I am getting my information—not until the time is right.

Nico never got a chance to answer: my bedroom door flew open and in walked a goddess of a woman. She was rocking a navy crop top and skin-tight white jeans. She had beautiful, long black curls that were past her waist; full, kissable lips; and violet eyes like Nico. Oh God! It hit me like a freight train— she's Nico's sister, but she is also the lady in the painting that was hanging in Randall Cane's office.

"Melakai was never yours to love. Your feelings are what clouded his judgment and got him killed." There was so much venom and hatred lacing each and every one of her words, but I couldn't stop staring at her, wondering why a portrait of her was hanging in Randall's office.

"Sophia, that's enough. Ryan didn't cause Melakai's death, you know this." Nico addressed his sister like she was a young child.

"Do not try to soothe me, brother, your *pet* knows what I say is the truth." Did she just call me a fucking pet? That's it, she didn't know me and she sure as fuck didn't get to stand there and pass judgment and blame me for things that were not my fault.

I had enough guilt over Kai's death, I didn't need her rubbing salt in my wound.

Standing from the bed, I make my way over to her, only for Nico to jump to his feet and block my path. I glare at the beast of a man. Being this close to him made me feel things I shouldn't; his proximity made my head go cloudy. He was like a drug to me. I wanted to touch him and let him hold me again. I wanted him to kiss me. I couldn't go down that road, so I leaned my head around his shoulder so I could look his sister in the eyes.

"I don't care if you are some fucking princess from a different world, you do not get to come in here and blame me for Kai's death. He would never have been with Randall if it wasn't for you getting your ass kidnapped." She recoiled at my harsh words, and Nico flinched, and I regretted the words as soon as they flew out my mouth.

"I'm sorry, that was harsh. I should never have said that."

"Don't ever apologize for saying what you think; you will be an honorable queen and good match for my brother." This woman is fucking crazy! One moment she hates me and wants to kill me, and now she is looking at me with respect. Clearing his throat, Nico spoke.

"Ryan meet Sophia. Sophia meet Ryan. I wish you both had met under better circumstances, but I guess luck was not on our side." Ignoring his introduction, I asked Sophia, "Why did you say Kai was never mine to love?"

"Because you were always destined to be Nico's, not Kai's."

"How could you know that?"

"I have premonitions."

"So you're a seer, like Aurora?"

"No, she can see future events and past events. I can only see people's love lives. I know, it's a crap gift to have, but it helped Nico." I pull my stare from Sophia to look at Nico, gauging her meaning from him. He gives nothing away, as usual. His eyes are burning with desire, and I would be lying if I said that one look didn't make me feel like melting on the spot.

"So, I guess I will just see you guys later then."

Nico and I don't acknowledge his sister's departure; we just stand there staring at each other. I don't know how long we stand there rooted to the spot but he is the first to pull his gaze away. I make my way back to the bed and sit down, trying to calm my racing heart. Nico reclaims his seat by the window.

"My sister is...she...she can be a lot to handle. Her time away from the fae realm has changed her." I could only imagine the horrors that Sophia went through at the hands of Randall Cane. Randall was a disgusting, vile man, and to make it worse, he now has my sister by his side. She and Randall want to use my blood to seal the fae realm. My blood is also the key to allow vampires to walk in the daylight. Unlike full fae blood, where you have to constantly top up, one drop of my blood is all it would take for a vampire to walk in daylight for eternity.

The only way to defeat Randall and my sister is to unlock my fae side, I'm an anomaly, half fae and half witch. Randall killed Jackson's father and drank his blood, the blood of an alpha.

We think he was the one to kill my father, for his blood as well. Randall drinking the blood of the alpha and the blood of my dad—a great warlock king and the best damn king the Knox has ever had.—means their power would run through his veins, making him stronger than almost everyone, except for me.

"I could only imagine the type of horrors she has had to endure at the hands of the Vampire King." Nico has a faraway look in his eyes, almost like he is reliving the torture of not having his sister by his side. "Nico, I need you to tell me the truth, please. Why were you so mad when you found out about Kai coming to me in my dreams?" With a deep breath, he looks me dead in the eyes and shatters me with his words.

"Melakai was never supposed to have a relationship with you; he was supposed to kill you."

Nico

I see the moment she processes my words—her face falls and her beautiful hazel eyes with the peculiar yellow ring start to glisten. I fucked up big time, and I know I have just broken her heart more than any person has ever done before. I just told her that the man she *thinks* she loved was meant to kill her, not love her. She was never his to love, and he fucking knew it; he betrayed me by seducing her and making her love him. My blood starts to boil as I think about his conniving ways, and I clench my fists, trying to control the rage coursing through my veins.

"Thank you." What the fuck is happening here? Did she just thank me?

"I don't understand? Why are you thanking me?"

"Because for the first time, you haven't lied or given me half-truths. You were honest. I appreciate your honesty, even though it hurts me. Can you please explain why Kai was supposed to kill me?"

This strong, beautiful woman has endured so much in her life, and yet here she sits, accepting every burden placed on her. She is the most beautiful creature I have ever met in my life. Her long brown hair is falling over her shoulders, I would love to tuck those strands behind her ear and whisper sweet nothings to her. She deserves my honesty, and I must do what I can to earn her trust back, before I break it again.

"I wasn't lying when I told you that I could never harm you, personally. Dom had gotten a message to Kai not long after I met with your father that day in the park; we told him about your blood and what it could do. We knew, no matter what we had all been through, Kai would never let our world die or let Randall and his vampires get your blood so they could walk in the sunlight. If vampires were allowed to roam free at all hours, they would cause mass havoc on the humans. So he offered to take care of it for us. Kai made a vow to your grandmother that he would protect her child, but he never vowed to protect the child's children. When Kai realized it was you who had the blood to seal my realm, he went rogue. He got a message to us months later saying the job was done and the problem was solved. Years went by, and by the time I figured out what this nagging feeling was in my chest, Kai had already made his move on you."

"I was sixteen when I first met Kai, and in the vision Aurora showed me, I must have been eight or nine. So Kai watched me for years."

"Yes, I only figured out what the feeling was in my chest because you and I are linked."

"Wait, we're linked?"

"Yes, love. I bound your powers so part of me remains inside of you." She opened her mouth, but I raised my hand to stop her. "Let me explain, then I will answer any questions you have, okay?" She gave me a stiff nod and I stifled a grin. My little spitfire didn't like to be silenced.

"I felt your fear and then I felt your...*need*, when Kai first came to visit you. I am aware that Melakai didn't attend to your *needs* until years later. I can feel when your emotions are heightened or when you are being..." I couldn't bring myself to finish the sentence.

"You mean to tell me you could feel every time Kai and I were *intimate*?" I couldn't form the words, so I just nodded. She blushed immediately, pushed up off the bed, and started pacing. I was coming to learn that she did this a lot when she was stressed or overthinking. "What am I supposed to say to that, Nico?"

"Nothing at all, love. It was never meant to happen. I didn't even know that it could happen until it did."

"What the fuck does that mean?"

Obviously I sounded like a blabbering idiot. I needed a second to collect my thoughts so I could explain this better. After a moment of silence, I felt composed enough to continue.

"What I'm trying to say is I didn't know I would feel your emotions or anything else. I only realized I could when you were scared or hurt or..." I knew the moment it clicked—she whipped around, glaring at me. I hung my head in shame, unable to meet her eyes.

"Stop, I don't want to hear anymore."

"I'm sorry."

"You're sorry. You're fucking sorry?"

She continued pacing, and I knew she wasn't done yelling or being angry with me. She had every right to be pissed; I knew and had done nothing. I left her there, when I could have saved her. I was a coward. I sat on the sidelines and watched, never once intervening, fearing that if I helped her she would eventually turn against me. She has the power to kill my people, and I left her to suffer at the hands of her mother because I was scared of what she could do to me. If she was this angry now, learning this, she was going to light me on fire when she found out what I had done *recently*.

"All the times I felt like I was being watched, I thought it was Kai. It wasn't, though, was it? It was you this whole time. When I felt like I was being watched at Randall's manor, it wasn't Kai. That was you." I nodded.

"You saw my mother and me, didn't you?" Again I just nodded. "Why, Nico?" I don't know if she meant to voice her last question, she whispered it so low, but I heard.

"Because I am a coward. I thought if you didn't know who you were, you couldn't hurt my people. Then things changed."

If this was a cartoon, steam would be blowing out of her ears. She stood directly in front of me now, hands on her shapely hips. I slowly raked my gaze up her luscious body until I landed on her eyes.

"What changed?"

"My feelings for you."

She laughed, I mean a full-on fucking belly laugh, with tears streaming down her face. I was stunned. Her reaction was not the one I expected, that's for sure. After a minute or so she finally got herself under control, glare firmly back in place, and I knew she was about to rip me a new one. My balls may have shriveled up in self-defense.

"Your feelings for me? Don't fucking make me laugh. If you felt anything for me you would have helped. You're right, Nico, you are a fucking coward. Did you like watching her beat me?"

I growled in response. I fucking hated every minute of seeing her being hurt, but I still did nothing to stop it, so I have no defense. "Did you like it when she couldn't pay and got her dealers to beat me? How about when she would lock—"

I couldn't take it. I jumped to my feet, and to her credit, she didn't shrink away or flinch; she stood her ground. We were so close I could feel her heat. She was so tiny the top of her head only reached my chest. She craned her neck back so she could look me dead in the eyes, and those full, beautiful lips were calling to me like a siren. I wanted to capture her bottom lip and nibble on it like I had done so many times before in her dreams. I reached my hand out and clasped the back of her neck. She tried to hide the effect I had on her, but she failed—I saw her eyes roll slightly and felt the shiver that went down her spine at my touch. She may be angry with me, but she also knew my touch could relieve the tension in her body and make her mind relax for a while.

CHAPTER 5

Ryan

His touch was like fire, and my body felt so hot and needy from his close proximity. I couldn't think with him being this close to me. I was hurt, *so hurt,* from what I had just learned. Looking into his violet eyes made me feel things I shouldn't feel. Kai had just died, and here I am begging Nico with my eyes to kiss me or fuck me. I was trying to shake myself out of my thoughts and pull away, but I couldn't.

I was a prisoner, and he had the key to release me. His eyes kept jumping from my mouth back to my eyes; he was contemplating whether or not he should kiss me.

I wanted him to kiss me. If he did, I could escape my thoughts for a while. I knew I could get lost in Nico; he constantly hurts me with his lies, but he was the only one who could mend me.

Nico was slowly leaning down, so close I could feel his breath on my lips. I snaked my tongue out to moisten them and his eyes followed my movement, his eyes turning so dark they were almost purple.

I knew that look, Nico was turned on. He closed the gap

between us with no hesitation and began exploring my mouth; as soon as his tongue entered, I let out a moan.

This was my first *real* kiss with Nico, and holy shit did it put my dream kisses to shame.

We explored each other's mouths, and for the moment, nothing in the world seemed to exist except for the two of us.

He ran his hands down my arms and to my hips, pulling me even closer. I gasped, but he didn't let me break the kiss. I could feel his erection pulsating against my stomach, and a sense of pride flowed through me, knowing that I was the one who had done that to him. This god of a man was turned on by little old me. His hand continued down to my ass and then to my thighs. He gripped the back of my legs, lifting me, and I instinctively wrapped my thighs around his waist and circled my hands around his neck. Holding him like this, and him holding me, felt right. I felt safe and protected, which was ludicrous considering he just said he watched me be beaten for years.

Nico started walking us back toward my bed, I wanted him inside me for real, it was all I could think about right now.

A throat clearing made Nico stop in his tracks. We both pulled apart and turned toward the bedroom door, where Dom, Jax, Alex, and Chase stood. I could feel the heat making its way up my neck to my cheeks. Fuck my life—my cousins looked pissed, Jax looked hurt, and Dom looked happy. There was an awkward silence for a beat until Dom spoke.

"Since you don't want to put her down, caveman, can I join you?" Nico started growling at the same time Jax smacked the back of Dom's head.

"Put her down now, *Tinkerbell*." I could tell from the tone of Chase's voice that he was mad I was in such a compromising position. I tried to wiggle out of Nico's hold, but he wouldn't budge, instead gripping my ass harder to make sure I couldn't move. I placed both my hands on his cheeks and turned his face so he could look me in the eyes.

"Let me down, big man." Nico didn't release me; he just continued to stare and nuzzled his face more into my hands.

"Yeah, put her down now, *big man*." Chase was being a sarcastic ass. When Nico didn't immediately put me down, I saw, from the corner of my eye, Chase taking a step forward. Nico quickly put me down and then pushed me behind his back, shielding me from the others. A part of me swooned at his protective instincts, while another part was pissed he wanted to protect me now, and not before.

"Take another step closer and you will regret it, *witch*." He did not just threaten my cousin. I tried to move around him, but he just kept blocking my path.

"Move away from her now, *Tinkerbell*." Oh God, did Chase really just call the king of Farrarie a fairy, *twice*? The others started laughing, but Nico didn't find it funny, judging by the way he went stiff as a board and stood even taller, if that was possible. I needed to defuse this situation now before we had a brawl on our hands. While Nico was distracted—glaring at Chase, I assume—I quickly stepped around him, only for him to reach and grab my arm and haul me back into his chest.

"Let her go Nico, now!" This time it was Dom, and I've never heard him use such a harsh tone before. Nico reluctantly let me go after a moment and then slumped down into the single chair. I didn't have time to process his actions before Chase was barking at me.

"What the actual fuck, Ry? Him? Seriously? Of all the fucking people, you go for Tink."

"Chase, please stop. I don't need to justify my actions to you."

"Yeah, I'm just here to worry about you when he breaks your heart like the last one did. Guess what, though? This time it will be worse, because you have to marry that piece of shit." Shocked, I reeled back like Chase had just slapped me. Chase didn't wait for a reply; instead he stormed out of the room like a fucking toddler. His words hurt. I didn't mean to piss my cousin off. This was all so confusing, and it was fucking with my head. One minute I hated Nico and then the next I was grinding on his dick while he carried me to bed.

"He didn't mean it, Squirt. He's just worried about you, and doesn't want to see you get hurt. I'll go talk to him and meet you later for our meeting." I gave Alex a forced smile before he left the room, shutting the door on his way out. I stood rooted to my spot, head spinning. Guilt was starting to eat at me now. Chase was right; Kai is gone, and here I am trying to jump Nico at the first opportunity. I felt someone place a hand on my shoulder and looked up to see it was Jackson. He held so much warmth in his chocolate brown eyes. He looked so young, but he was nearly triple my age. Being a supernatural had its perks, I guess.

"Take it from someone who thought he had a mate, but was tricked by his real mate. Love is complicated, and both of those boys love you dearly. Seeing you so torn up about Kai, and you shutting them out, has been hard on them. They just want to be there for you." I felt like a complete asshole now; Jax was right—I holed up in my room since learning about Kai and never once have I given any thought to how my cousins would be feeling. I was such a selfish bitch.

"You're right, Jax, I'm gonna go see if I can find them and talk to them." Jax gave me a gentle squeeze on my shoulder and then released me. I nodded to Dom as I exited the room, but I didn't utter a word or turn back to Nico. I was confused and ashamed at the way I had just acted. What the hell is wrong with me, and why can't I fight this pull I have toward Nico?

As I walked down the hallway, I turned right and found both my cousins arguing. When they spotted me, they stopped their bickering immediately. I didn't have any words, so I just walked right up and engulfed Chase in a hug. It took him by surprise, and after a beat, his arms came up and wrapped around me. He rested his chin on the top of my head.

"I'm sorry, Ry. I didn't mean what I said, it's—"

"Shh, Chase, it's fine. I know you are hurting, and I know a lot has changed for both you and Alex. I am the one who is sorry; I let my grief cloud my judgment." Chase and I pulled apart and I hugged Alex, as well, telling him how sorry I was. They both waved away my concerns and we made our way toward the game room; it had pool tables, air hockey, ten-pin bowling and TVs. We wandered over to one of the many couches and took a seat.

"Squirt, we are here because we want to be and not because we have to be. Chase and I could have easily gone with Stevie but we didn't. We believe she is wrong." I appreciated what he was saying. It meant a lot to know that they chose to come with me instead of having to.

"I just want you both to know that I am so thankful to have you here with me. I couldn't do any of this without either of you." Chase looked like he swallowed a lemon; I could tell he wanted to ask me something. "Just ask whatever you want to know, Chase"

"How did you know Tink was lying, and how did you know he was the one you have to marry?" *Shit.* Taking in a few deep breaths, I unburdened myself and told them the truth and what my *secret power* really was. I needed to trust in them, that they would have my back. This was new for me. I have never had anyone who would risk something or was even willing to choose me before.

I didn't look up when Ryan left the room. I couldn't. I could tell Jax and Dom both stayed behind, but I couldn't look at them either. If I did, they both would know the truth.

"She's your *hugacko*, isn't she?" Trust Dom to put the pieces together. I heard Jax's sharp intake of breath. Well, now they both knew.

"Does she know?"

"No, I haven't told her. I don't want that to have any sway in her decision." I knew as soon as the words left my mouth they were both going to be pissed.

"You need to fucking tell her, Nico! She has a right to know."

I stood and marched over so Dom and I were toe to toe. I needed him to see the look in my eyes.

"It is my burden to bear, not yours."

"So you're just going to lie to her *again*?" Jackson needed to learn how to keep his big mouth shut for once.

"This is none of your business. Stay out of it Jackson. I mean it."

"Or what, Nico? She has been through enough, and I have

had enough of your shit. I was just coming around to forgiving you, but after the stunt you pulled with switching Ryan for Aurora, I want nothing more than to rearrange your fucking face." I sighed and scrubbed a hand down my face, then made my way back to the chair and dropped down. Jackson was right; I was fucking everything up because I was scared. I would never admit that to them, though.

"What do you suppose I do then, Jackson? I never meant for my spell to make you think Ryan was your mate. I would never trick you like that; it was only supposed to mask Aurora's scent."

"I understand why she asked you to do it. I'm still pissed that you did it, though. You both could have come to me."

"No, she can't Jax. You know as soon as the spell wears off and you scent her, you will want to claim her. She doesn't want to be claimed; she's not a wolf." Dom was right, every wolf that scents their mate is overpowered by the need to claim and mark them as their own.

"Enough about me and my fucked-up love life. We should go grab a bite to eat and then get ready to meet the others." I was not looking forward to this meeting. I somehow had to convince Ryan that she *wanted* to marry me.

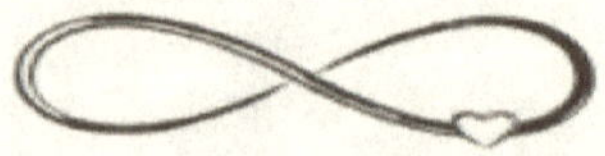

After getting something to eat in the mess hall and catching up with a few of Jackson's pack members, we started to relax in our chairs. It was just the three of us now, and I started feeling nostalgic. We used to hang out all the time and just talk shit and have fun, and now our foursome is a threesome. It was hard to wrap my head around Kai being gone. I was angry as hell at him; he had no right to go behind my fucking back and trick Ryan. She had no right falling for him, either; her heart needed to stay out of it when it concerned him. She was mine, whether she knew it or not. Kai was the safe one, and I was the one you took a gamble on. I would never be the one to hold your hand and make you think everything was okay. I am the one who will push you and tell you to just do it. Snapping out of my somber thoughts, I turned to face my brothers, ready to try mend things, until my sister ruined it.

"Why are you three sitting here like there isn't about to be a war?"

"Sophia, what an unpleasant surprise, as usual."

"Dominic, be seen not heard. No one wants to hear your bark." Sophia and Dom were always bickering at each other, even before Sophia was taken by Randall. Now they didn't even try to hide their loathing for each other; They used to be so close, and now they couldn't be in the same room without trying to hurt the other in some way.

"Cut the shit, you two. What do you want, Sophia?"

"Nothing, Jackson. I just wanted to make sure that I wasn't going to be left out of the meeting you are planning with the half-breed." Jackson started growling at my sister, and I had to defuse this before she went hurricane Sophia on their asses. My sister had a temper on her even before her ordeal.

"How do you even know about that, sister?" No one knew about the meeting except for us, Ryan, Alex, Chase, and Aurora. My sister was always sneaky, it seems over time she has honed her skills.

"I have my ways, brother. I want in on the meeting." Before I could even answer, Dom did.

"No, you're not invited."

"I'm not asking, and if you want information about what Randall is planning, then you will have me there." *Shit,* she had us there. She turned before any of us could respond and left the mess hall.

"Well, I guess Sophia is coming to the meeting." Dom didn't look pleased at all about my sister joining us, but I didn't have time to dig into what was wrong with him.

We made our way to Jackson's office, and as we rounded the corner, I spotted Ryan, Aurora, Sophia, and Ryan's cousins leaning against the wall outside of Jackson's office.

"I thought I told you not to be here." Who the hell was Dom snapping at? Dom was the most chill and relaxed one out of all of us. To see him so uptight and angry was slightly unsettling.

"Oh, Dominic, since when have I ever listened to a word you have said?" Sophia had an evil smirk plastered on her face, and her eyes were shooting daggers at Dom. Dom marched right up to my sister, leaving barely an inch of space between them, I tensed, ready to intervene if things got out of hand. I would not let anyone hurt my sister, no matter how difficult she was. She has been through enough.

"How about you start listening now, little dove?" *Little dove?* Since fucking when did Dom have a pet name for my sister? He and I would be having a little chat about that after this meeting. Sophia flinched at the nickname.

"Dom, that's enough. Sophia has information we need, hear her out." At Aurora's words, Dom took a reluctant step back from my sister, muttering something under his breath about *pain in the ass* and *never listens*.

We all entered Jackson's office, each taking a seat except for Soph, who stood staring out the window. No one spoke for a good minute or two; I avoided eye contact with Ryan as best as I could. The tension in the room was stifling. No one wanted to push Ryan, but we were running out of time. Before I could get lost in my thoughts any further, Sophia spoke.

"How long before her powers are unlocked?"

"The *her* is sitting right here, thank you very much," Ryan snapped. She hated people talking about her instead of to her.

"Okay, everyone chill out. We're all on the same side here, and we all need to work together." Alex the know-it-all told us off like we were children.

"Well, since you clearly have it all figured out, little Knox, why don't you fill us in?" I knew I was being a condescending prick, but I didn't give a shit. Alex was annoying.

"Actually, Nico, I do have it figured out. Since it is a binding ceremony of two races and two members of royal bloodlines, all leaders will need to be present for this, including Randall." What the fuck—since when? How did I not know about this? I looked at both Dom and Jax, both of them had the same look of shock, so I'm not the only one who didn't know then. "Judging by the look on all your faces, none of you knew about this"

"Don't be smug boy, it's unattractive" at least Sophia found her voice because Dom, Jax and I were still in shock. I looked over and saw Aurora with her head down and shoulders bunched, something was wrong.

"Aurora, are you okay?" she looked up and tried to hide the fear etched across her face, now I was really worried. What the hell happened to put that look on her face.

"I.....I...um...I" she couldn't even string a sentence together. Jax got up from his seat and rushed over to her kneeling down in front of her. He tried to grab her hands but she snatched them away. He fell back on his heels but didn't move.

"Aurora, can you please tell us what happened?" I had never heard Jax speak to anyone like that. He was so calm and soothing, like he was trying not to spook an injured animal. He knew Aurora was his mate, but because the spell hadn't worn off yet, her scent was still masked. Everyone knows it's only a matter of time before Jax pounces on her. She took a few deep breaths and then looked directly into Jax's eyes.

"If Randall has to attend the wedding, then so does Ryan's sister." I heard Ryan's sharp intake of air. She didn't want to face her sister, yet. "Tyler will come with them as well." Ah, so this was about her traitor of a brother. Tyler betrayed us all when he decided to help the enemy, but I imagine his betrayal crushes Aurora worse than anyone.

"I know this must be hard for you, love. Tyler made his choice. No one blames you."

"Everyone hates me! the whole pack has turned against me because of my brother. I was already an outcast because I can't shift, and now this?" Jackson was growling and starting to shake; he needed to get his emotions under control before he shifted and hurt Aurora, being that close to her. Dom and I jumped to our feet at the same time and rushed over to Jax, while Ryan was pulled to her feet by both her cousins and went to stand by Sophia. I placed my hand on Jax's shoulder. *Worst mistake.*

CHAPTER 7

Ryan

Jackson turned and snapped—I mean, full on went to bite Nico. Nico quickly jerked his hand away and stepped back. Jax was shaking and trying to take deep breaths. His hands were turning into claws. I gasped. Jax spun toward us and his eyes had turned yellow. He started growling again. He took a step in our direction, and I froze. Nico jumped in front of Jax, shielding us from his view.

"Brother, you need to calm down. Aurora is safe, and she's here with you now." Jax didn't reply; he just stood there, staring at Nico. Hair burst from the pores of his arms, and long gray hair was present on his legs, too. Jackson was going to shift, and I felt like I was going to piss myself. "Aurora, you need to talk to him; you're the only person he is going to listen to at the moment."

Aurora raised from her seat, no sign of fear on her face at all. She didn't even seem nervous. She made her way over to face Jax, and Nico stepped aside so she could take his place. She tentatively reached out a hand and placed it on Jax's cheek, and he looked down at her. I felt like we were witnessing a private moment between two lovers.

"Jax, sweetheart, I'm gonna need you to calm down and take a deep breath for me." At the sound of her voice, Jax started to relax, the fur on his arms and legs lying down and beginning to retract. I swear Aurora is an animal whisperer. No one moved or spoke for fear of setting Jax off again. Aurora took a step back from Jax once it looked like he had himself under control. She took the seat she vacated and tapped the spot next to her for Jax to join her. He didn't hesitate; he made his way straight over to her and plonked down, sniffing her and rubbing his cheek against her head. Dom gestured for the rest of us to take our seats and we did, except for Sophia, who remained by the window. I was seated between Alex and Chase, Dom took the spare spot next to Jax, while Nico took the single seat.

"I'm sorry for my outburst, I normally have better control of my wolf," Jackson said, voice still gruff with wolf. I felt sorry for him; you could see in his eyes he was embarrassed for his loss of control but pleased that Aurora was now tucked firmly into his side.

"Don't worry about it, brother, we all lose control sometimes." Dom seemed to always know the right things to say, bless him.

"Let's move on and get down to business shall we?" Clearly Nico was sick of the interruptions. I couldn't really blame him, because I want to get this over with as well—the suspense is killing me.

"What are the first steps for Ryan?"

"The first step Chase is that Nico and Ryan need to marry." Well, Aurora doesn't beat around the bush, does she? I couldn't help my next words—sarcasm is my go-to in serious situations.

"Yay, I'm going to be a teen bride, how cool." I felt at war with myself over this situation: part of me felt sick for being forced into marriage, but another part just felt...numb. Resigned to follow a path I didn't choose. I don't know how I'm supposed to feel, honestly. Nothing has gone right for me in the past few weeks. My sister has gone rogue, my dad died—murdered, though I didn't know that originally—and Mom is fuck-knows where. I don't have a home anymore. The only thing I do have is my truck, which is still parked at Stevie's. I have no idea what the hell I'm supposed to do. I didn't notice Nico had moved until he knelt down in front of me. He didn't touch me but just stared into my eyes. And for a moment, I got lost in the depths of those beautiful violet eyes.

"I know this all must be hard for you, love, believe me. I have been around for a really, really long time, and I have never married. This is all new to me too. I don't know how to be a husband, or if I will be any good at it, but you have my word I will try my hardest, and when that isn't enough, I will try even harder. I will treat you like the queen you are and cherish you daily. You will be loved by me and want for nothing."

Nico's words stirred something in me. I didn't know what this feeling was. It almost felt like hope. I knew Nico meant every word he said, and call me a fool if you like, but I believed him.

A thought entered my head at that moment, telling me I was lucky it was Nico I had to marry and not some weird old guy in a suit.

I leaned forward and placed my hand gently on Nico's cheek. I don't know if he meant to but he pushed into my touch, almost like it soothed him. I was scared and unsure, but deep down I knew Nico wouldn't let me fail or fall. As much as I tried to deny it, he really was the same man I spent hours laughing with and talking to in my dreams. I did know Nico. I just didn't know him properly, while I was awake.

Taking a deep breath to steady my nerves, so I wouldn't fumble my words when I spoke, I said, "I hear everything you are saying and I believe you will do all of those things. I just need you to be patient with me. I will do my best to be all the things you need me to be." I feel like I should tell him that I know his secret, but then I would need to answer his questions of how I know and I wasn't ready to reveal my answer yet. Both my cousins knew how I was getting my information.

"Okay, well, now that Nico is on one knee and just proposed, I think we can start planning the Faeling wedding of the year!" Dom seemed excited for this wedding, and that made me feel uneasy. I could tell he was up to something.

Nico stood and offered me his hand, and I hesitated for the briefest moment before gingerly placing my hand in his, letting him pull me to my feet.

There was a small gap between us, and I could feel my body wanting to gravitate toward him. It took a lot more restraint then I wanted to admit to stay where I was and not close the gap between us.

Looking me in the eyes and never breaking that contact, Nico asked the others to give us a minute alone. Everyone except Chase and Alex readily agreed.

Those two bozos left the room grumbling about jackasses and rich-dicks. When the door clicked shut behind them, Nico led me over to the window Sophia had been staring through earlier.

The view from Jackson's office is stunning; you can see the forest and mountains that seemed like they went on forever. I could sit here gazing out at Mother Nature all day; I found it so calming. Jackson told me the compound was built in the middle of their lands so that no one ventures near their living quarters. I guess it wouldn't be a good idea to live close to town, in case humans saw them in their wolf forms. Nico's homeland was beautiful as well, and also a wooded retreat from the world. At Nico's loud exhale, I snapped from my thoughts and turned so I could see his face. He was still looking out the window.

"I shouldn't even be saying this, but you can still turn around and run, love. You owe my realm nothing. You owe *me* nothing. I'm a selfish bastard, I admit that, but I would never force you to marry me. Do I want to marry you? Yes, I do. But you're so young and have your whole life ahead of you. If we marry, you will be expected to return to Farrarie with me and rule by my side. You will be Queen."

Fuck, I didn't think of any of that. I would have to leave my realm and live in his. Though, it's not like anyone here would miss me, aside from Alex and Chase.

I would have to leave everything I know and move to a whole different world. Part of me was scared shitless and another part was longing for the adventure that move would bring. It would be a new beginning for me, a fresh start where no one would know of my past. I could start over.

"As scared as I am with this whole unlocking my power thing and marrying you, I could never let innocent people die due to my own fear. I don't want to have to do this, Nico—any of it. In a short amount of time I have lost two people I care about, one is dead and the other might as well be. The point is I will not let my fear overshadow what I am supposed to do. If I have to marry in order to stop my sister and Randall, I will. I promise you, your world will not die because of me. I will do everything I can to protect your people, and I will try to be the best queen I can be." I could see pride shining in his eyes at my words; it meant a lot to see that look and made some of the tension in my body dissipate.

"Hearing those words means a lot to me, love. I will help you with training and be there with you every step of the way." I knew he meant every word. Nico grasped my hand and led me over to the couch, where we both took a seat and quietly sat with each other, hands clasped. I don't know how much time passed, but we were both pulled out of our moment when the others re-entered the room. No one said a word, but I did notice both Chase and Alex were apprehensive at seeing me sitting with Nico instead of rejoining them. They took their seats on the other couch, with Sophia now taking my normal spot between them. Dom sat on my other side, and Jax and Aurora each took one of the single seats.

"Right, so let's get down to business. I'm guessing by the way you're holding his hand now, Ry, that you are okay to go ahead with this sham of a wedding." Before I could snap at Chase, Alex did it for me.

"Brother, if you can't support our cousin and the great sacrifice she is making, then you need to get the fuck out of here." I have never heard Alex or Chase speak to each other like that; to say I was shocked is an understatement. Judging by the look on Chase's face, he was just as surprised. He kept opening and shutting his mouth like a fish out of water. I could tell he wanted to say something, but no words would come out.

"I...I don't know what to say to that."

"You're not supposed to say anything, Chase, you're just supposed to nod your head and agree with me. I know this is hard, but we need to support our cousin. She needs us." Hearing those words from Alex gave me a rare feeling of belonging. I would miss these two the most when I left for Farrarie.

"Thank you, Alex. Nico and I have decided that we will continue on with the wedding. Our feelings about this mean nothing in comparison to a whole world dying." Nico gave my hand a squeeze, letting me know that he supported me, which was good, because I was going to need his support to get through all of this.

Everyone then launched into plans for the wedding. It wouldn't be anything huge, just something small and intimate.

We didn't have enough time to plan a huge wedding, anyway, and we didn't want a lot of people there in case Randall or Stevie tried something stupid, which seemed likely. We agreed the wedding would take place in four days' time.

After a couple hours of planning, we all decided that we were happy with the outcome. Everyone had their own jobs to do in order to make this wedding happen. We would be run off our feet for the next couple of days, that's for sure. Nico and I haven't broken the news to my cousins that after all this stuff with Randall and Stevie, that I would have to move to the fae realm. I was not looking forward to *that* conversation. I knew my news would hurt them and they would worry. We all decided to make our way over to the mess hall and grab some dinner. After that I planned to retire and enjoy a nice long soak in my claw foot tub in my en suite.

You could hear muffled sounds of everyone talking and laughing as we neared the mess hall. Thank goodness that room was sound proof I could only imagine how loud the noise would be if it wasn't. Jackson was leading our group, so he was the one to push the doors open for us to enter.

As soon as we did, everyone's laughter and conversation stopped. Awkward much? Sophia didn't seem to notice, or she just didn't care—she pushed past us and made her way over to the buffet counter and started to dish her food.

Alex and Chase followed. Nico rested his hand at the small of my back and gave me a gentle push toward the others. I felt like his hand was burning through me, the way his touch set me ablaze. Trying to push my focus away from the feeling of Nico touching me, I started counting in my head how many steps it takes to get to the counter. Conversation seemed to resume once we had taken our seats, and no one approached us, which I was thankful for. I ate as quickly as possible and excused myself with the explanation that I was tired, but I really just needed to dream.

CHAPTER 8

Nico

I know she is hiding something, but I can't figure out what. Her cousins know her secret, I'm sure of it. They never questioned her exit, and they *always* questioned her whereabouts. I needed to figure out her secret; she knew things she shouldn't. Before I could get more lost in my thoughts, a bread roll hit me in the side of the head, snapping my gaze to the left and glaring at the asshole who dared to throw anything at me. I wasn't surprised to find the asshole was none other than Chase. The prick had a smug smile on his face that had my hand itching to slap off.

"Now that I have your attention, your *majesty,* what do you really have planned for your wedding with my cousin?" He's a smart fucker, I give him that, but I couldn't let on that I had ulterior motives for my wedding day.

"I have no idea what you mean, little witch." His playful expression dropped immediately and his eyes turned dark. That's right; let your magic out to play, young one, so I can teach you a real lesson.

"You may think you have my cousin fooled, *King.*" I was getting sick of having the words *king* and *majesty* thrown at me like they were vile terms. "But you are wrong; we are already two steps ahead of you. You are the one playing catch up to our plan." Alex stood and placed a hand on his brother's shoulder, and Chase reluctantly stood and followed his brother out of the mess hall. To say I was confused was an understatement. I knew she was up to something, but if Dumb and Dumber were that cocky about their plan then she must be planning something big.

"Was it just me or did they just say they have a plan of their own and we are not privy to any of it?"

"I hate to say it, but I think you're right, little dove. I believe our little Knox coven has their own plan." Sophia and Dom were right; they are the best at finding out secrets. They always have been. It is a hidden talent of theirs. Apart they are good at solving mysteries, but together they are unstoppable. My little witch and her cousins are hiding something big from us, and we need to find out what it is.

"I think we should..." I couldn't even finish my damn sentence before my sister cut me off.

"No, whatever you are thinking, it is wrong. Aurora and I will go and speak with the witch alone. She will not disclose anything to you, brother. You have lied and hidden things from her, and she needs allies. Aurora and I will be that for her." Dom and Jax both looked apprehensive about this plan, but we really didn't have a choice. Sophia stood and nodded for Aurora to follow her. Both of the girls exited the room without even glancing back or waiting to see if we agreed or not.

"I guess I'll say it, then; those women have you both by the balls."

"And So-So doesn't have you by the balls, Dominic the Great Sorcerer?" said Jackson. *Wait a fucking minute.*

"You have feelings for my sister?" I was burning a hole in the side of Dom's head with my glare, but he wouldn't tear his gaze from Jax's. I slapped my hand on the table, which garnered the attention of the others in the room, but I didn't give a fuck at this point.

"Answer me now, Dom!"

He finally pulled his gaze from Jackson's to meet mine, and we sat there staring at each other for a long moment. Dom wasn't giving anything away; he was the hardest person to read. Jax was an open book—his eyes told you his emotions. Dom hid his better than anyone I knew.

"Of course I care about her, Nico. She is like a sister to me. Do not ever question my affection for her; you know as well as anyone I love her. I have always cared for her as much as you." I felt like there was a double meaning to his words, but shouting broke out across the room and distracted me.

"Alpha, the traitor is at the border! He wishes to speak with you." Jackson, Dom, and I all jumped to our feet and rushed toward the young man who had shouted the news.

"Is he alone?" Jax had his alpha voice on now; he wasn't asking for the truth—he was pulling it from his pack member. Jackson is one of the strongest alphas I have ever met in my time, with the exception of Dom.

"No, Alpha. He has four vampire guards with him."

With a curt nod from Jax, the young man turned and hustled out of the hall. We followed Jax outside and toward his border, at least twenty other pack members following us. They would never leave their alpha, and if Tyler tried anything on Jax, the pack wouldn't hesitate to take Tyler out. Once we neared the border, I could see Tyler and four others, like the young boy had said, but the four of them were carrying something big. My heart dropped when I caught sight of the item they were carrying.

"You are either stupid or suicidal for coming back here, *Beta*." Unsurprisingly, Jax was still bitter and angry about Tyler's betrayal. Tyler winced at Jax's words.

"I have not come here to fight or to die, Alpha. I have come to return something that belongs to you, and then I will leave."

"Why would you come here, knowing that we could kill you?" His behavior seemed inexplicable.

"Because, your majesty, not everything is as it seems. I mean you all no harm—I just want to do the right thing." The four vampire guards stepped forward to hand over the huge, rolled-up carpet, and four of Jax's pack members stepped forward and collected it for us. Tyler turned to leave when Jax stopped him with his words.

"Aurora's my mate." Tyler didn't turn or tense.

"I know, Jax. I've always known. So has she. You will make her strong, and she will make you stronger. Treat her well and love her like she should have always been loved. Trust in her and prove to her that you are worthy of her, and I promise you she will give it up to stand by your side." Jax stood there gaping at Tyler's retreating form, clearly lost for words. I think we all were. Aurora has clearly known she was Jax's mate longer than she let me believe.

After Jax finally gathered himself, we made our way to the compound and to one of the spare rooms. Once inside, we made our way over to the bed, the carpet was unrolled and the contents were revealed. I owed Tyler for the return of my brother's body. Looking at Melakai, lifeless, covered in bruises and cuts, nearly brought me to my knees. His fingers were broken and nails were torn off, and his ankle was snapped and laying at an odd angle.

"I will fucking kill them for what they have done." I could feel the anger radiating off Dom, the need for vengeance thick in the air.

"None of them will make it out of this unscathed, brother—I vow that to you." Jax was right. Anyone who had a hand in doing this to our brother would not live.

"We will avenge our brother." We would make every one of them pay. Just then the bedroom door burst open and all three of us spun around, shielding the intruder from being able to see Melakai.

"You have five seconds to move, all of you, or I will make you." How the hell did Ryan know we were here, and how did she know we had Kai?

"How did you know he was here, love?" I'm glad Dom asked the obvious question, as I was still too shocked to form words.

"I told you all before, I have a secret power." Her cousins, my sister, and Aurora then filed into the room as well. My gaze shot to my sister, who just nodded, telling me to give Ryan what she wants. Reluctantly, all three of us stepped aside to let Ryan see Kai.

There was no look of shock, or any emotion at all, which was worrying, to say the least. She stepped forward and made her way around to the side of the bed and perched on the edge, gently placing her hand on top of Kai's battered one and using her other hand to caress his cheek. Due to my little bond with her, I could feel her sorrow and heartbreak.

"I'm glad you got here safe. Now I think it is time for me to tell the others the truth." Jax, Dom, and I looked to the others, and they seemed to be clued in on what was about to happen, which set me on edge. Chase, the smug prick, smirked at me. I tore my gaze from him and focused on Ryan. I needed answers, and she was about to give them to me, whether or not she liked it.

"What is the truth, love? What are you hiding from us?" *From me.* She took a few calming breaths before she answered.

"I will tell you everything, Nico."

After I left the mess hall, I made it back to my room in record time. I quickly made my way over the bed and grabbed the small vial Alex had given me. Without hesitation, I drank it and laid down. A short while later I was being shaken awake. I blinked a few times, trying to get my eyes to focus, and when they did, I saw both my cousins standing by the edge of the bed.

"Did you do it? Is it done?"

"Yes, Alex, he's coming to us now."

"Okay, we need to be ready. Are you ready to tell the others the truth?"

"Yeah...I think so, Chase. I understand a lot more now, and when he is woken he can help me understand more. He is a key piece in this war; I needed the others to think I was scared and uncertain about marrying Nico blindly or else they would have asked too many questions. Nico is very bright, and he would have caught on to my lie, or Jax would scent the lie or some shit. I know you don't like it, Chase, but I do still have to go through with this wedding."

Chase didn't comment, just nodded his head. He didn't like

Nico and that was okay, but I did need him to be cooperative while we fought this war.

A few minutes later there was a knock at the door, and before any of them could answer it, the door opened and in walked Sophia and Aurora. These belonged on a runway, they both had bodies to die for. To say I was shocked that they were in my room, would be an understatement.

"Yes I know, I'm the last person you thought would come to see you. Just know that Aurora and I both know what is about to happen. She has seen it and I was the one who cast the spell, I didn't know if it would work but clearly it has."

"Wait, you knew this whole time and said nothing?" I could hear the shock in my own voice.

"Yes, it wasn't my story to tell. I owe Melakai my life; he saved me from the torture I endured every day, and he knew setting me free would cost him his life. I did the only thing I could." Wow, color me purple and call me Barney! Sophia has more fucking layers than an onion.

I could feel him. I knew he was here. I told the others it was time. None of us said a word on the walk to the room where the guys had brought Kai. Aurora led us there, knowing which room Jax would use to hold the body of his fallen brother.

I slammed the door open—nothing like a grand entrance—and strutted into the room. All three of them were staring, their faces slack with shock. I felt pretty fucking cool to be the one surprising them for a change.

"You have five seconds to move, all of you, or I will make you." My words were harsher than I intended them to be, but time was of the essence.

"How did you know he was here, love?"

"I told you all before, I have a secret power." It was the only answer I could give Dom at the moment. I moved past them and made my way over to the side of the bed. I ignored all of Kai's injuries and placed my hand atop his cold one, my other hand caressing his hollow cheek. He was so cold and stiff; I hope I wasn't too late. "I'm glad you got here safe. Now I think it is time for me to tell the others the truth."

"What is the truth, love? What are you hiding from us?" What Nico really meant was what am I hiding from *him*.

"I will tell you everything, Nico—after." I knew the guys deserved an explanation but right now, I didn't have the time.

"Later, brother. Alex, you and Chase get her what she needs. Aurora, draw the blinds and close the door." A moment later Sophia was sitting on Kai's other side, holding his other hand. "Thank you" was all she whispered. A little while later the door opened, and Alex and Chase came in with the dagger and spell. They made their way toward me when Nico blocked their path.

"You are not going near her with that blade."

"If you don't step aside, *Tink*, I won't help her save the dirty leech." I flinched at Chase's words. Kai wasn't a dirty leech; he was a good man. Kai may have led me astray for years, but his reasons were noble, in a way. Dom pulled Nico out of the way, and the boys quickly made their way to my side. I grabbed the dagger and the spell paper from them. I have never in my life cast a spell, but the boys assured me I could do this. I *had* to do this. He told me to trust him, and I did. We needed Kai alive so he could fulfill his role in our plan. I hope Kai didn't hate me when he learned I had double- crossed him. I knew it was wrong of me to do this, but I had no other choice. I just hoped Kai saw it that way, as well.

"Wait, what are you doing, Ryan?" Blowing out a breath, I turned to face Jax and answered his question.

"I'm going to try and bring him back." I heard Jax, Dom and Nico all gasp; I know this must be hard for them to believe.

"You can not bring back the dead, babe. He won't be the same, trust me." I know Dom is scared, but he didn't understand.

"He isn't dead, per se." Dom snapped his head toward Sophia.

"What the fuck are you talking about, little dove?"

"I cast a spell. I didn't know if it would work, but apparently it did. That's why Ryan is trying to revive him with her blood and the spell she has in her hand." I mouthed a silent *thank you* to Sophia for explaining what I couldn't; the lump in my throat was preventing me from saying anything at the moment.

I gripped the dagger in my left hand and pressed the blade to my right hand, slicing my palm. I winced at the pain. I have never cut myself on purpose before, so I was shocked at the pain. I placed my right hand across Kai's lips, letting my blood drip into his mouth, and began to chant the words written on the paper.

"*Revivera ma soulty inuguta, revivera ga parsona. Revivera ma soulty inuguta, revivera ga parsona. Revivera ma soulty inuguta, revivera ga parsona.*" I kept chanting, over and over. Minutes went by that felt like hours. When Alex placed his hand on my shoulder, I snapped my lips together and turned to face him. His beautiful baby blues held so much pity in them, and my eyes began to fill with tears. I could feel the tension in the room rising. The spell and my blood didn't work! I thought it would work, and banked on it working so Kai would be with us again. I failed. I failed Kai, and I failed everyone. I removed my palm from Kai's mouth and placed it on his hand, not caring that my blood was still dripping everywhere. I looked at Kai's beautiful, ashen face and whispered a final goodbye. I stood, ready to leave, when my right hand was gripped. I spun around and saw Kai's hand covering mine. No one spoke or even moved —we just stood there and watched for a moment. Kai's eyes started to blink ever so slowly. I held my breath, praying he would come back to us.

"Holy fuck, he's...he...I think he's waking up." I assume it was Dom who spoke. I couldn't tear my eyes from Kai for even a second to check. I didn't want to miss seeing him come back to us. After a few minutes, finally Kai opened his eyes, and I had never been happier to see those beautiful gray-blue eyes in my life. I gently sat back down beside him and rubbed my hand across his cheek. He turned his head slightly my way and our eyes locked. I could feel his love for me pouring through his gaze. *Oh, you really would have been the better choice.*

"I just contacted the pack healer. He's on his way, and I got another bringing in some blood bags." That is so cool that Jax can communicate with his pack through their mind link. Focusing back on Kai, who hadn't taken his eyes off me, I spoke.

"Welcome back, big guy. I thought we had really lost you there." Kai tried to speak but ended up in a coughing fit and groaning in pain. The healer arrived at that moment, pushing us all out of the way and barking orders at the two ladies with him.

"Hello, Melakai. I am Dr. Jeremy. I'm going to take a look at your wounds and try to see what I can do to help. I'm going to give you some painkillers and run an IV of blood, then I need you to try and relax." Kai grunted in response. Two men I haven't seen before came and made their way over to the doctor. "I need you both to hold him down while I realign his ankle."

"He's a vampire. He can heal on his own." Dom was right; I forgot vampires and shifters could heal on their own.

"The spell that was cast must have slowed his healing abilities. I need to reset the break before it heals at an incorrect angle." Oh, okay, that made sense now. But it sounded awful. We all left Kai's side to allow the doctor to do his job. Everyone spread around the room and sat in chairs or on the floor. Occasionally one of us would pace to pass the time, and the others would chat among themselves. Hours passed, but none of us would leave the room. We didn't want Kai to be alone. I could feel Nico's gaze on me, but I was a coward, and I couldn't face him. I knew I had a lot of explaining to do, and I knew he would be angry with me for keeping this from him, but now everything made sense for me. My feelings for Kai were never my own, but my feelings for Nico, they *were* all my own. I still loved Kai, but just not in the same way I used to, more like a brother or best friend. Ugh! I shouldn't say brother—that was fucking gross, considering the shit we did together in my dreams.

It was late by the time the doctor was finished with Kai, and I was fucking exhausted and needed sleep stat. The doctor treated all Kai's wounds and dressed them with gauze. His ribs needed to be wrapped, as he had broken most of them.

His ankle was in a splint and resting atop a mound of

pillows. The Dr said he should be fully healed by the afternoon. That would be great, as my wedding was fast approaching.

We still had so much to do. Jax had tasked his pack members with making the necessary arrangements for the ceremony, Nico was bringing a fae minister from his realm, and Aurora was organizing my dress. Alex and Chase were saddened that the Knox coven wouldn't be attending one of their heir's weddings, but I couldn't help that. Stevie was their queen, and I was just a stranger to them.

I was shaken from my thoughts when I heard the bedroom door close. The doctor and all his helpers were gone; it was just us now. Jax, Dom, Nico, and Sophia made their way over to Kai. Aurora and Chase followed them. Alex offered me his hand to help me to my feet, as I was sitting on the floor. I gladly accepted, and we followed the others over to Kai.

Kai already looked better and had some color back in his face. The blood bags must have really helped; the cuts on his face and arms were already starting to heal. I reached out gingerly and ran my fingers through his beautiful blond hair. His eyes fluttered open at my touch. His gaze zeroed in on me and remained there. I smiled, trying to reassure him without words that he was going to be okay and that I have forgiven him. One day soon I would be the one asking for his forgiveness.

"I'm glad you're okay, big guy. I'm sorry it took me so long to cotton on to your messages."

"You have nothing to be sorry for, mi amor." His voice was scratchy from disuse. The torture he endured at the hands of my sister and Randall made me sick to my stomach. How my sister could change from being one of the most caring people to a monster still baffles me.

"It's good to have you back, brother." Kai pulled his gaze from me so he could look at Jax.

"Thank you, brother, it's good to be back. I didn't think the spell would work, but I'm glad that it did." Kai turned from Jax to Sophia. "Thank you So-So, I owe you my life." Tears started to cloud in Sophia's eyes, but she quickly blinked them away. Sophia didn't seem like the type of woman who cried or let anyone see how she was really feeling. I admire that about her.

"You owe me nothing, Kai. After everything, I would say we are even." Dom and Nico shared a look and judging from their expressions, they hated not knowing the full story of what happened to Sophia. Nico's eyes told me that there was so much rage simmering beneath the surface. He wanted revenge for what happened to his sister. I could be wrong, but Dom was giving me the same vibe.

"I'm glad you're back, Kai, but I have to know how this is even possible." I knew Dom was trying to be patient and not push Kai for an explanation straight away, but there was only so much he could handle. Dom was one of those people that had to know the full story about everything. Before anyone could speak, I answered for Kai.

"Why don't you guys grab some seats and get comfortable. It's a bit of a long story." Everyone settled themselves around the bed, waiting for Kai and me to explain.

I'm sitting here, staring at her and the way she is running her hand through Kai's hair. Since when did she stop being angry at him and when the hell did they become friendly like that? I knew they were *close* in her dreams, and just thinking about Kai having his hands on *my* woman made my fucking blood boil. I hate the way I'm feeling, like I'm some insecure child. I have never felt like this before about anyone. I hated Kai just for having her hands on him.

"Could you stop fucking touching him? He's alive, yay! That doesn't mean he needs you to constantly fucking pat him like he's your pet." I snarled, shocked at my own outburst. I saw the others staring at me with wide eyes. Dom and Jax both looked like they wanted to laugh. I narrowed my eyes at them until they looked away. I returned my stare to Ryan and found she was glaring at me. The look she was giving me told me that she was about to lose her shit. Oh, great, here we go. I'm about to get my ass handed to me, again.

"Get off your fucking high horse, Nico. You have no right to tell me what to do. We may be getting married, but make no mistake—this is a business transaction and nothing more," Fuck, her words hurt more than if she just stabbed me. Schooling my features so she couldn't see how much she hurt me, I went to answer her when Jax spoke.

"Don't kid yourself, love, you know I can tell when you're lying." She went beet red. I forgot about Jax's secret talent of being able to detect lies. His little talent would come in handy for this conversation. She was glaring daggers at Jax.

"Tell them everything, mi amor, they have a right to know." She moved her eyes from Jax to me and I saw her swallow. Time to fess up, baby.

"Okay, after Nico and I returned from the dream where we saw Kai die, I thought the same as all of you, that he really was dead. After I awoke that day, I was alone, but I started hearing a voice. I honestly thought I was going nuts, but then I was pulled into a daydream. That has never happened to me before with Kai or Nico." She was blushing. Aw, my little spitfire was embarrassed. I hated hearing her mention that Kai was present in some of her dreams as well.

"I only see the guys in my dreams at night. Anyway, once I was in my daydream, I saw Kai. Needless to say, I was shocked and happy, because I thought even if he was dead, I could still see him, you know." I couldn't help the growl that slipped out. It pissed me off to know she was still seeing him when she clearly had feelings for me. "Easy, tiger—it's not what you think."

"What is it that you think I am thinking, love?"

"If you let me finish, Nico, then you will understand," she snapped, like I was a petulant child. "Back to the story then. I saw Kai, and he told me he was still alive. I didn't believe him, of course, I thought it was my subconscious playing tricks on me. After talking with him and hearing his explanation, I started to hope. He told me a spell had been cast to slow his healing, so that it would appear like he had actually died. Kai also told me that Randall would want to gloat about killing him, so he would make sure that his body was returned to you guys."

"That doesn't explain how you knew that your blood and that spell would bring him back." Dom hated not having all the answers, and right at this point in time I couldn't agree with my brother more.

"When I cast the spell, Kai asked me to make Ryan's blood the key to return to the living. The spell to revive him was passed onto Alex and Chase by Kai through Ryan."

"You don't have enough power to cast a spell like that, Sophia." I didn't mean it as an insult, but from the way my sister stiffened, I knew that was how it came across.

"You have no idea what I am capable of, *brother*. The trials that I have had to face have made me stronger. I am no weak half-breed anymore." The conviction in Sophia's voice was slightly unsettling, but I didn't have time to sit here and pull her words apart.

"So-So, that's enough." I turned to glare at Kai. How dare he speak to my sister like they were long-lost siblings! She wasn't his sister, she was mine!

"You do not get to butt your nose in my affairs, Cane, she is my sister, not yours!" I saw the look of hurt cross his face before he quickly masked it and nodded.

"Don't you dare sit there and throw around insults like that! You may be a king in Farrarie, but you are not in your realm now. You do not get to speak to people like they are trash. Do I make myself crystal fucking clear, brother?" Everyone in the room stopped and turned their gaze to my sister. I was as shocked as the rest of the group. Sophia has never, I mean never, spoken to me like that before. I wasn't angry at her for her outburst—on the contrary, I was fucking proud that she had found her spunk or backbone or whatever you want to call it.

"Well, fuck me sideways till Sunday, babe. That little

outburst was so fucking hot!" I leaned over and slapped Dom up the back of the head. "Dude! What the actual fuck was that for?"

"That's my sister you are fucking flirting with. You are never to talk to her like that," I hissed.

"Calm down, King. She is a grown-ass woman and can decide who she wants to spend her time with." I was about to slap the stupid smirk off that dumbass warlock Chase's face.

"Calm down, everyone! All of you need to shut it and listen! We do not have the luxury of time. You and Ryan get married in three days time." With that reality check from Aurora, everyone shut up and sat back in their chairs and gave Ryan their full attention.

"The reason I could be the key to bring Kai back is because his blood still lingered in my system. After the blow up at the cabin and Randall biting me, Kai gave me his blood to help heal my wounds—" Melakai cut Ryan off before she could finish explaining.

"I asked for Ryan's blood to be the key because one, I knew that she would be with you all. Two, I trusted her to return me to the living. I am sorry, brothers, but with how things have been between us, especially between you and I, Nico, I didn't know if you would want me to wake up. There are a lot of sins I must atone for, but I am ready to move forward."

"But you said you could never go against the blood oath you have with Randall." The know-it-all warlock Alex had a point.

"The spell Ryan asked you to acquire is a death spell, as well as a reviving spell. What that means is the spell kills me then restarts me."

"What exactly are you saying, Kai?"

"What I am saying, So-So, is I could never make you the key to bring me back, because you would never have completed the spell Ryan did. You are far too loyal; you would never have gambled with my life."

"You knew he could have died and you still fucking did it?" My sister was angry, and she started to make her way over to Ryan but was stopped by Dom. How the fuck did he move so fast?

Dom was right in front of Sophia, blocking her path. She didn't try to move around or make a sound, just simply lifted her hand and placed it on his chest.

Dom flinched.

Why was he flinching at her touch? Before I could ponder that thought any more, a bright yellow light shot from the hand she had placed on Dom's chest, and he went sailing across the room before he smacked into the wall beside the bed, cracking the plaster. Jax was quick enough to move out of the way so he didn't get crushed. Everyone was on their feet, trying to find a safe place to stand for the presumed showdown. Dom was quick to recover and was back on his feet. I quickly jumped in front of her, trying to stop this battle between her and Dom.

"Enough, Dominic, you will not hurt my si—" I couldn't even finish what I was saying before Dom fucking used his magic to freeze me. I couldn't move or speak. I was lifted by his magic and placed to the side. He must have done the same to everyone in the room because no one was moving or speaking. I could see him making his way over to my sister, but she didn't move or cower. She squared her shoulders and lifted her chin. Fuck, she really has changed. The sister I knew would be hiding behind me, crying, begging me to save her. Dom's eyes were glowing a bright purple; they only did that when he was really pissed off. Sophia knew that and I'm guessing that's why she is smirking at him.

"You think it's funny, little dove, to launch me—me, of all

fucking people—across the room? If you were anyone else, Sophia, I would fucking end you."

"But I'm not just anyone else, am I, Dominic? Oh, that's right. We don't talk about that, do we? You just hide behind your power and lie through your fucking teeth!" What the fuck is my sister talking about? "You deserve so much fucking worse. You're a fucking coward, Dominic Silver."

I could immediately sense the change in Dom. He never really shifted anymore; only when he absolutely had to. His wolf was huge and a born alpha. Jackson and Dom had tried to shift together many times, but every time they did, their wolves went at it. Jax was an alpha by birth, and Dom was the son of an alpha. Dom is stronger than any wolf I have ever met. He and Jax are both evenly matched, and if Dom shifted now, I guarantee Jax would shift also. They would both be slaves to their beasts in the fight for dominance, and they would tear this room apart. Dom was shaking and taking deep breaths, trying to calm down so he didn't shift. He must be focusing hard on trying not to change into his wolf and putting all his energy into that, because we suddenly found ourselves able to move again and speak. I rushed over to my sister to grab her and move her out of the way. I was just about to grip her hand when she pulled it away. She never broke eye contact with Dom while she spoke to me.

"If you touch me, brother, he will shift and try to kill you. You need to move back with the others and stay there until he calms."

"I am not leaving you, So-So, never again. Slowly move toward me and then stand behind me." Dom was growling now, I could see his eyes had changed from violet to gray-silver.

"Touch her and I will fucking kill you, Nico!" Dom growled through clenched teeth.

"Nico, move away from me now. If you don't move, he will

shift and take you and Jackson out. He hasn't shifted for months; his wolf will go rogue and block our Dom out." I was torn; I didn't want to move in case Dom hurt her, but then I didn't want to make the situation worse by not listening.

"Nico, can you please come here and listen to Sophia?" I turned to Ryan, who was pleading with her eyes as well as her words. She was a siren to me, and I had no choice but to listen and move away from my sister. I made my way over to her and stood beside her, at the head of the bed, next to Kai.

CHAPTER 11

Ryan

I was standing between Nico and Kai. Kai was trying to sit up to assess the situation better. I placed my hand on his chest and shook my head. With a huff, he laid back down and didn't try to move again. Sophia and Dom were still standing in the same place. Jax, Aurora, and my cousins were standing on the other side of the bed. Jax was standing slightly in front of Aurora, ready to shield her if Dom did shift.

"Deep breaths, Alpha, I don't want to have to throw your wolf around as well." Dom laughed at Sophia's words, which is what I guess she was hoping for, as some of the tension in his back and shoulders started to ease. He wasn't fully calm yet, but a lot calmer than he was a minute ago. His laughter stopped abruptly, and tension returned to his body.

"You're right, Soph, I deserve so much worse. I will spend my life making it up to you, I swear." Wow, since when did Dom have a remorseful side?

"I can't forgive you, Dominic, I have tried for years."

"Forgive him for what, Sophia?" Nico had his big brother voice on now, and fuck, it was hot. Shit! I had to get my head out of the damn gutter. Sophia turned her gaze to her brother while Dom seemed to stiffen.

"It doesn't matter, Nico. It was a long time ago."

"It matters to me, little dove."

"Why the fuck do you keep calling my sister *little dove?* What the fuck is going on between you two?" Nico was pissed. Anyone with eyes could see that there was something going on between Dom and Sophia. When they thought no one was looking, one would stare at the other. Nico was so blind to not see that there was history between his best friend and his sister. You could tell neither of them wanted to discuss this, so I did the only thing I could think of.

"How about we table that debate for another time and get back to planning a wedding and talking to Kai?"

Everyone agreed and started to situate themselves around the room again. Well, everyone but Nico, who still stood and glared at his sister and Dom. Jax brought a chair over for Nico so he could sit, but Nico ignored his friend's gesture. I sighed and grabbed Nico's hand, and that seemed to have shocked him out of his glaring match.

"Come on, big guy, sit down." I gently pulled my hand from his and pushed on his chest till he was sitting. I turned to head back over and sit with Kai, but before I could move an inch, an arm snaked around my waist and I was pulled backward till I was sitting on Nico's lap.

I turned to glare at him and tell him what I thought of his macho man display. The words died in my throat when I saw his eyes. He was battling his anger and trying to control his control freak urges by not demanding answers from Dom and Sophia, and if me sitting on his lap was what was going to help him calm down, I would endure this torture. Well, I would make him think it's torture. Inside I was swooning like a school-girl at the close contact. I loved having Nico's hands on me. I felt safe and secure. I loved when he would whisper sweet nothings in my ear when we were in my dreamland. A throat clearing had me snapping out of my thoughts and looking straight at Jax.

"Um...shifters have great noses, love..." I didn't know what that meant. Nico was chuckling behind me, and now Dom was too, but at least he was trying to hide his laughter behind a fake cough.

"Okay?"

"I mean we can scent when people are happy, sad, angry, hungry, turned on..." Oh fuck no. Nico and Dom both started laughing, I turned beet red and looked to Kai for confirmation. He nodded. Oh my God, they could smell my arousal. I went to quickly stand but Nico tightened his grip, his laughter stopping immediately.

"I could have gone my whole life without knowing that my cousin was turned on, fuck you very much, jackass." Kill me now. I couldn't even look toward Chase; I was embarrassed enough without having to hear his comment.

"I think Ryan has suffered enough, let's move on, shall we?" Bless you, Alex.

"I have to say, at least we know she will be okay with consummating the marriage," Dom commented, and Jax slapped the back of Dom's head. "Dick, would all of you fuckers stop hitting me? It's fucking starting to piss me off."

"Stop saying dumb shit and then no one would hit you," suggested Kai, and we all turned to stare at him. He hasn't weighed in on this discussion much, so I think we were all shocked to hear from him. Everyone started laughing, which helped lighten the tension in the room and make everyone feel more comfortable.

"I'm sorry I lied to you all, I couldn't risk telling anyone except for Alex and Chase. I needed them to handle the spell for me." I was lying through my teeth. I told them to grab the piece of paper from my room; it had the spell *he* told me to use on it, not the one Kai said to use.

"I would like to continue to move ahead with the wedding planning and making sure everyone is on the same page with Randall and my sister being here." At the mention of the vampire king and my sister, everyone seemed to tense up and sit straighter in their seats. I knew my time was running out on avoiding my sister.

"Mi amor, you can do this—" Nico cut Kai off.

"I think Ryan and I need a moment alone with Kai, if you guys don't mind." Alex and Chase didn't move an inch, Dom and Sophia seemed reluctant to act. Jax and Aurora watched the lack of action with interest.

"Why would I leave my cousin alone with both her stalkers?" Fuck, Chase was exactly like Dom, they both needed to filter their words.

"Because soon enough she will be my wife, and I won't be asking next time, I'll be *telling you*." The balls of Nico to speak like that to my cousin! I turned so he could get the full effect of my glare.

"Do not treat me or speak about me like I am some property to be owned! I will not let you dictate my life, married or not."

"I will make any call I see fit for your safety and what is in your best interest, with or without your permission, love. I won't ask for forgiveness or permission. That is not in my make-up. I am King. It is my right."

Hell to the fucking no! He did not just pull the *I am King* card! I've had enough of his bullshit. Just when I think he is starting to understand me, he goes and does some stupid-ass caveman shit like this. I have been controlled my whole life, and I will not let anyone control me again. I pushed his hand away and stood, but of course Nico couldn't let me have the dominant ground so he stood as well. We were chest to—well, his chest to my head, so I had to take a step back and tilt my head to glare at him. He was glaring back.

"You are a stubborn-ass bastard is what you are, Nicky boy, and I have had enough. We all know what needs to be done to prepare for the wedding, so I suggest we all should hop to it before I kill the fucking groom!" I turned away from Nico and made my way over to Kai, pecking a kiss to his forehead and ignoring Nico growling behind me. I told Kai I would come back later and check on him, thanked the others for their help, and left the room. I didn't spare Nico a glance on my way out.

Once again, I walked down so many different hallways that I got lost. This place was so freaking huge it would take me years to learn its layout. After another five minutes, I finally found a door that led to the backyard, where there was a beautiful garden. There were beds of roses and wildflowers. The garden seemed like it went on forever, so I began to walk to try clearing my head. I had so much going inside me that I didn't even know where to begin. The first thing I knew I had to do was talk to Nico and tell him everything about what happened with Kai and how I came to know certain things. Part of me felt like I finally got some form of closure with Kai, now that I knew the truth. Yes, it sucked to hear it, but it helped me move forward from what I thought I had with Kai. I knew, deep down, from the moment I found out Nico was real, he would be my future. I have never admitted this to anyone, or even myself, but if there was a man I would want to marry, it was Nico.

I loved who I became when I was with Nico. I felt stronger and brave. I have never stood up to anyone the way I stand up to Nico; he pushes me to want more and to strive for better things. I decided right then that after my walk, I would find Nico and we would talk this shit out. I wouldn't marry him while we were both angry at each other. As I was rounding a corner, I stopped in my tracks when I heard very familiar voices bickering.

Bending down, so I could peek around the corner of the building, I saw Dom and Sophia arguing. I know I shouldn't be eavesdropping, but I wanted to know what the deal was between these two. The chemistry between them was off the fucking charts, and the sexual tension was even worse.

"How many times do I have to say I'm sorry, Soph?"

"You can say it a thousand times more, Dominic, and I still won't forgive you."

"I tried to find you!"

"You didn't try hard enough!"

"I fucking went ape shit, Sophia, I hunted through the whole of Farrarie and Earth for you. I didn't know that asshole had taken you until Kai told us."

"Don't you dare blame this on Kai! He was the only one who fucking helped me. You have no idea what that son of a bitch did to me every fucking day. He knew hurting me would hurt my brother. He never loved Ryan's grandmother; he is *incapable* of love. He let his own wife be beaten and raped by his men. What do you think he let happen to me, the sister of his greatest enemy? I was used and tortured more than you can even imagine. Do you know—"

"Stop! I can't...I...*please!* I will fucking kill him, Sophia. I swear to you, I will make him pay."

"I will be the one to put a stake through that fucking pig's heart!"

I quickly turned so I could sneak away but I ran straight into a solid wall. Before my scream could come loose, a hand clamped over my mouth and I started to panic.

"Shhhh, love, it's just me." I relaxed instantly at the sound of Nico's voice. He removed his hand from my mouth and then placed it on my lower back, guiding me back toward the way I came. When we were far enough away from Dom and Sophia, he asked, "How much of that did you hear, love?"

"More than I should have," I answered honestly. He grunted but didn't comment on me spying on his sister and Dom.

"I want to take you somewhere, if you will let me."

"Nico I appreciate the offer but I just..."

"Give me an hour, please." It wasn't often Nico said please. Interesting.

"Since you said please..." We both chuckled at my reply. "Where are we going?"

"It's a surprise. I'm going to open a portal so we can get there faster." I didn't argue, and we continued to walk toward the woods. A couple of minutes after we reached the tree line, we came upon a clearing. Nico removed his hand from my back and stood in the center of the clearing. He was whispering words under his breath and then a portal appeared. I don't think I would ever get used to this whole magic thing, it was always a sight to behold. Nico reached a hand out to me and I placed my hand in his without hesitation and stepped into the portal. It felt like we were being sucked in by a Hoover! Once we stepped out the other side of the portal, I gasped.

Nico had brought me to my favorite place on Earth, the *real* Lake William.

CHAPTER 12

Nico

I heard her gasp as the portal closed behind us. Was that gasp because she was happy I brought her here, or was she pissed off because this was the place Kai had brought her, and where she thought he died?

"Nico, I…I—" Dammit, I made a huge mistake bringing her here. I bowed my head, feeling defeated, letting my black hair hang over my face, shielding my eyes. Nothing I do seems to make her happy. Instead I have a knack for pissing her off.

"I'm sorry, I'll take us back now." As I turned around to open another portal, she grabbed my hand. My eyes shot to hers. She had a beautiful, shy smile on her face, and her eyes told me what she could not. She was glad to be here, but unsure what her next move would be.

"I'm shocked you brought me here. I have never been to Lake William before. Well, of course I have, but only in my dreams. I didn't even know this place was real until recently."

I couldn't stop the grin that crept across my face. I made her happy by bringing her here! I am going to take that as a big win. She grasped my hand and led me along the small trail toward the lake's edge. Once we got to edge, she let go of my hand, kicked her shoes off, and shuffled closer to the edge of the bank, easing down and letting her feet dangle at the water's edge. I followed her lead, though I must say I can't remember ever doing something so mundane. There is little time for such things when you are a king. We sat in comfortable silence for a while, just gazing out at the lake and the mist-wreathed mountains. I can see why she loved this place so much. Alaska was one of the most beautiful places here in the Earth realm.

"You know how I knew about Jax not being my mate?" I turned to look at her; her long brown hair was hanging like a curtain, shielding her face from me. I leaned over and gently tucked it behind her ear so I could see her profile. She sucked in a breath at my touch and I smirked. I loved how my touch affected her.

"I have an idea," I answered.

"If your idea is that Kai told me, you're wrong." I stiffened.

"I don't understand, love. If it wasn't Kai, then who was it?" She took a deep breath and then turned so she could look me in the eye.

"My dad. He's been coming to me in daydreams as well."

"How long has this been happening?" Randall Knox was dead. The only way for him to be able to come to his daughter was if his remains were never properly consecrated back to the earth, or so I have been told.

"Since we arrived in Alaska."

"Why didn't you say anything?"

"I didn't know what it was at the beginning. I only started to think they were real and meant something when I met Kai and then you. After we left you in Farrarie, I started to pay more attention to my daydreams, in case they were real, you know?" She turned and focused her attention back on the lake, and I did the same.

"I understand what you are saying, love. So when Kai came

to you and you realized that he was still alive, you thought that maybe—?"

"That maybe my father was alive?"

"Yeah"

"I really wished that was the case, but my father told me that there was no way he could come back. The thing with Kai coming back is a once-in-a-lifetime kind of deal. He also told me that Kai would play a big part in the coming battle." I reached over and grasped her hand in mine, locking my fingers through hers. I knew that reality had to hurt even more after losing her sister.

"Have you told any of the others about your father coming to you?"

"No, I wasn't ready to share this with anyone. I didn't even tell Kai or my cousins." Knowing that I was the one she trusted with this information meant so much to me.

"Thank you for your trust."

"Wow, the great Nicholas Stone is thanking a common witch." We both chuckled at her attempt at a joke. After a few moments of silence, I asked, "What part does Kai have to play in this war?"

She took too long to reply, so I turned and saw that tears were rolling silently down her face. I pulled my hand from hers and wrapped it around her shoulders so I could pull her close to me. She leaned her head on my chest, and I wrapped my other arm around her and tightened my hold. We sat like that for a while until her sobs slowed and she was able to get her breathing back under control.

"Kai can never return to Farrarie. He doesn't know. The spell I used cancelled out any remaining fae blood that may have lingered in his system. Kai thinks the spell killed him and then brought him back. In part he is right, except the spell killed his fae side. Kai is full vamp now."

"Kai has seen himself as a full vampire for a really long time now, love. He will not be mad at you."

"You don't understand, Nico. The spell my father told me to use has a failsafe against our kind." She said *our kind.* Hearing those words made something in my heart flutter. I was beyond proud.

"What are you trying to say, love?"

"If Kai ever steps foot in the fae realm again, he will go up in ash."

"No, love, I cast the spell on my realm to burn all vamps aside from Kai."

"Kai was made from Randall's blood, correct?" I nodded. I had a feeling I knew where she was going with this story, and I didn't like it. Farrarie was Kai's home. "The spell wiped all remains of *Kai's* blood from his system, so the only blood that remains in Kai's system is Randall Cane's." *Oh fuck.*

I felt Nico tense. Now he understood what I was trying to say. I knew Kai had hoped to return to his homeland after Randall was defeated, but now he could never go home. I abused his trust in me, and Kai was never going to forgive me.

"The spell you cast, though—Kai said he told you what spell to use. He would never use a spell that would block him from returning home."

"I didn't use the spell Kai told me to use."

"What? *Why?*"

I could hear the anguish in Nico's voice; he was devastated his brother could never go home. Even after their big falling out, Nico made Kai exempt from the spell he cast in Farrarie after Randall kidnapped Sophia.

"Because my dad told me the spell Kai wanted me to use would never work."

"There has to be more to it than that, love." Nico was smart enough to know I was hiding something else. Blowing out a breath, I forged on.

"We needed Kai to turn fully. When Randall falls, Kai is now a true heir to the vampire king. No one will be able to contest his claim to the throne. Melakai will be named King of all Vampires, through blood." I felt Nico stiffen, and his arms dropped from around me. I moved away from him and sat up straight, staring out at the lake. I was a coward and didn't want to face him.

"What have you done?" The sheer disbelief in his tone made me flinch.

"I did what I had to in order to ensure Kai returned to us."

"You took away his choice! Kai hates being a vampire, and now you have gone and made him a true heir to the race he despises most!" Nico was shouting now, and I wanted desperately to run away, but I couldn't.

"You wanted me to be open and honest with you, Nico, and that is what I am trying to do."

"I know, love—it's just a lot to take in. I think I just need time to process what you have told me." That was fair enough. I mean, I did just drop a bomb on him. I just needed to make sure that he didn't tell Kai before I had the chance to.

"Can you please not say anything to Kai? I will tell him, but I just need to find the right time."

"You have my word, love, but you need to tell him soon, before this war breaks out. I would hate for him to be blindsided by the news."

"I promise I will tell him soon."

"Can I ask you something?" I had been waiting for him to ask this question; I knew it was only a matter of time.

"Of course."

"What happened between you and Melakai? You seem different toward him now." There it is—Nico was very perceptive.

"That is a bit of a long story."

"I have nothing but time when it concerns you, love, in case you haven't noticed. After all, I did leave my realm to be run by my second in command so I could be here with you." I hadn't even thought of that. Nico was a king, yet here he was, in my world, trying to help me save his world.

"Nico, I'm so sorry. I hadn't even thought about what you've given up to be here."

"You're most welcome. Now can you put my curiosity to rest, please?" With a laugh, I began to tell him the truth.

"When Kai came to me in those daydreams I told you about, he said he may not make it and that I deserved to know the truth. He told me that he used his power of emotional control in the beginning of our relationship to manipulate my feelings for him. Don't get me wrong—I was attracted to Kai the moment we met." Nico started growling. He did that so often that I was starting to wonder if he was a shifter as well. "Kai only tried to manipulate my feelings for him because he wanted me to choose him."

"Why?"

"Because if I chose him, he would have taken me away from my sister and all this supernatural stuff, so I would remain oblivious to all this and I would never know what I was. If I didn't know what I was, then I could never be used by anyone."

"I get his reasoning, but I don't agree. You can't hide from what you are; you would have figured it out eventually."

"Kai also told me now that I know the truth, he and I could never be."

"You would never be his, love. You have been mine since we first met ten years ago." I ignored the fact that he was referring to when I was eight years old, because that was just creepy. "I can see the look on your face, and no I did not mean it like that. What I meant is that you would never belong to Kai because you are my *hug*—"

Nico was cut off by a portal opening behind us. He jumped to his feet so fast and yanked me up by his arms, positioning himself in front of me so whoever it was would have to go through him to get to me.

"Relax, brother, it's just me." How the hell did Dom know where to find us? Sensing there was no danger, I moved to stand beside Nico and smiled at Dom. "Hello, love," he said with his usual rakish grin.

"What is it? Why are you here, brother?"

"I thought you might like to know that Kai is up and moving about. We're all gathering in the mess hall to catch up before we call it a night. He said he has some things to tell us about Randall." Nico looked down at me with a regretful smile. Our little bubble of peace had just been burst. We both quickly put our shoes back on and Nico clasped my hand once more and we stepped through the portal.

After exiting the portal, the three of us went directly to the mess hall. Nico still had my hand firmly planted in his, and I didn't protest. I liked the feeling of him touching me. The whole team was here: Jax, Aurora, Sophia, Alex, Chase, and Kai, as well as two others I hadn't seen before. Once we made it to the table where they were gathered, the two newcomers bowed their head at Nico. Obviously they knew who *he* was.

"Ryan, this is Maverick, my right-hand man and commander of my army." Nico gestured to the burly man that had long, straight black hair and the most beautiful bright green eyes, they almost seemed like they were glowing. This guy was freaking huge—his arms were the size of a bear's. I smiled shyly and waved; this guy scared the shit out of me. Nico gestured toward the second man; he was tall and lanky, he looked like he was built more for speed and agility than brute strength. He had short-cropped brown hair that was shaved on the sides, and yellow eyes. I am guessing all fae had different colored eyes to humans, it would explain why I have a ring around my pupils. "Ryan, this is Larick, he is our spell master. He helps train our people in defensive and attack magic." That piqued my interest immediately.

"Hi!" God, I wanted to slap myself. I meet these guys, who are obviously important to Nico and the fae realm, and all I can do is squeak out a lame ass *hi*. Everyone chuckled at my obvious awkwardness.

"It is a pleasure to meet you, Your Majesty." Hold up—Larick just called me *your majesty*.

"Oh, I'm not a queen; my sister is the queen of our coven."

"I was referring you being the queen of Farrarie, Your Majesty." *Oh!* Before, when I felt embarrassed, that was just a taste of what I was feeling now. Now I was just awkward as fuck. What does someone even say to something like that? Nico saved me from responding by engaging the two in conversation about why they were here and not back in the fae realm training. I tuned them out and pried my hand from Nico's, taking a seat next to Kai. From the corner of my eye I could see Nico glaring daggers, but Kai either didn't see Nico's look or chose to ignore it.

"How are you feeling?" Kai looked much better, and a lot of his cuts had already healed. Kai still seemed down, though. I could tell he still had a lot on his mind.

"Much better now." Then crickets. Okay, so he wasn't in a talkative mood. I knew I had to witch up and tell Kai the truth about the spell, but right now didn't seem like a good time. So I chickened out and went with small talk.

"I'm glad you're back with us."

"Me too, mi amor." I felt weird hearing Kai call me *mi amor* now. I wasn't his love. Well, maybe I was, but he wasn't mine anymore. I felt a pain in my chest at the thought of losing another person.

Kai had been a huge part of my life, even before I knew he was real. Kai gave me someone I could talk to when things at home with my mother were bad.

Each night, when I went to sleep, I could escape to my dreams and be somewhere else, become *someone* else. My relationship with Kai has always been different to the one I have with Nico. Kai was the one who would listen and was gentle. Nico, on the other hand, would demand things and make me forget through the euphoric bliss of orgasms, until I forgot my own name. I could see now that the times in my dreams when Kai and I were intimate, that the spark and burning desire I felt for Nico was just not there. Don't get me wrong—I always felt need for Kai but only a base level, almost like I just wanted to feel good, so we would fuck.

When Nico and I have sex in my dreams, it's soul shattering and all consuming. Nothing else exists in that moment aside from the two of us. I'm embarrassed to admit that having sex with Nico became like a drug to me; I would crave the feeling of him each night and would find myself disappointed sometimes when I would arrive in my dream land to find Kai and not Nico. I am such an idiot that I did not realize sooner. A thunk on my head pulled me out of my thoughts. The culprit was a bread roll. I snapped my gaze across the table to glare at my cousin.

"I called your name like three times and you ignored me."

"I didn't freaking mean to ignore you, Chase, you big baby, I was thinking!" At my outburst, everyone around the table erupted in laughter.

I must admit it was nice to see everyone smile and laugh. It seemed to break the ice a bit, and we all started to talk about mundane things.

The girls wanted to know what it was like living in New Zealand and what foods we had there. We sat there for a few hours chatting and eating dinner and dessert. It was so nice to get to know these guys better; they may be a shifter, vampire, fae, or whatever else, but they were still people, and it was humbling to hear their stories of how they grew up and all that.

I tried to hide my fourth yawn, but Nico, the ever observant stalker, noticed and gave me a stern look which said *"go to bed."* I reluctantly stood and bid everyone good night. I was beat from the long-ass day.

CHAPTER 14

After Ryan left the mess hall, everyone continued to chat amicably about their lives. I noticed Kai had been very quiet for most of this. It was strange, considering he normally added his version of events when I, Jax, or Dom told a story of our youth. However, I didn't have time to worry about his salty-ass attitude —this might be my only time to ask Ryan's cousins some things about her. I made my move when there was a break in the conversation.

"Were Ryan and her sister close, even though they lived apart?" Both of the warlocks' faces dropped at the mention of Ryan's twin sister. Chase was quicker to recover from the shock and answer my question.

"Stevie and Ryan were closer than anyone I know. Even though they lived apart, they would always find a way to see each other or talk on Ryan's hidden cell phone. It would destroy Stevie when she couldn't speak or see Ryan because her mother was on one of her tantrums. Stevie and Uncle Ralph tried many times to rescue Ryan,

But Nina would always threaten to expose what we were to the humans. Uncle Ralph thought he had more time, and that when Ryan turned eighteen, she would be free to leave and go live with him and Stevie. But obviously that's not how it went." I hated myself more than I ever have, hearing her cousin recount her fucked-up childhood. I knew firsthand what she had gone through and never lifted a finger to fucking help her. Ryan was a beautiful person, and so forgiving. Even after she knew Kai was meant to kill her, she still saved his life and made sure he was okay. And I know she's suffering guilt at the loss of Farrarie for him. I mean, who fucking does that? A question from Aurora pulled me from my inner turmoil.

"If they were so close, why would they part now?" This time it was Alex who answered.

"Ryan didn't have a choice. She knew nothing about supernaturals. All she knew was that we were taking a family trip to Alaska for three months. The truth is we were supposed to arrive here and tell her about what we are and what she is, then introduce her to our coven and that was it."

"What changed?" Ahhhh, so Kai *was* paying attention, he just didn't want to talk.

"*You* happened, Melakai." Kai snapped his eyes up to look at Chase. "On our way from the airport to the cabin, Ryan had fallen asleep and had a dream, and she was calling out your name! That's when we knew we were too late, if you were already visiting her." Chase sounded pissed, and I couldn't blame him.

"I was never visiting her to hurt her—" Alex cut him off with a hand raised.

"All you do is hurt people, Melakai; it's what the King has trained you to do!" In response, Kai slammed his fist on the top of the table, the two of them locked in a glaring match.

"You think you're so noble because you went to see her every couple of months or called and text when you could? No, you are not noble! You are all fools. She would tell you she was fine and her mother wasn't home or she was studying in her room for a test. She fucking lied to you all!" I could feel the anger radiating off Kai, and I was starting to get the feeling I was going to hate the ending of Kai's story. "She was never alone; if her mother was out, she made sure one of her dealers was there to keep an eye on Ryan. If they got bored, they would beat her or humiliate her. Every night she went to sleep I would go to her to help heal her wounds; I could never fully heal her or her mother would have noticed. I only gave her enough of my blood to heal the worst of her injuries. I was her escape, not either of you or her fucking good-for-nothing cunt of a sister." Kai turned his glare my way then. I knew he was angry and he was about to unleash his anger on me. "As for you, Nico—you are the worst of them all. Your lies are catching up quick, brother. I suggest you start telling her the truth. I don't give a fuck what she is to you! I will always protect her, even from you!" I jumped to my feet. He'd gone too far now.

"You ever fucking threaten to take her from me again, Cane, and I will kill you where you stand you—" Kai cut me off.

"I never hid her worst nightmare from her and lied about it. You are a spineless piece of shit. Tell her the truth or I fucking will." *Holy shit, Kai knew.* I looked to Aurora, who had the same look of shock I did. We were the only two who knew about it, and now Kai does too. I am so fucked if he tells Ryan. I need to man up and go to her. "You have till the day of your wedding to tell her the truth, or I will tell her before she walks down that aisle."

Her cousins are both now fixated on our conversation. "What the fuck are you talking about? What are you hiding from my cousin?" Great, now her annoying ass cousins are gonna be sniffing around too. Dom and Jax were both shaking their heads. They knew I did something bad; they didn't know what it was, but they knew it wasn't good based on Kai's reaction alone.

"Say nothing to her, Melakai. I will go to her now and tell her everything." I didn't wait to hear any of their replies. I stood and left the hall, making my way to Ryan's room. I was dreading this conversation with her. I regretted what I had done, but I can't change it or go back in time. I need to own my mistake and try making it right with her. Perhaps if she lets me explain, maybe then she could forgive me, in time.

As I was nearing her room, I started to feel a familiar pulse in my chest. I was more accustomed to these feelings now after having to deal with them for years.

When I arrived at her room, I stood outside her door and strained to hear any sounds. All I could hear was her steady breathing; she was asleep.

I tried to open her door but it was locked. *Oh, little one, that won't keep me out.* I placed my hand over the knob and chanted an unlocking spell, and the door clicked open. I stepped inside, shutting and locking it behind me. She was lying on her side, with one leg in the covers and the other over the top. She looked so peaceful. As I moved closer to the bed, I noticed she was just in a shirt and panties, and my mouth watered. Her ass was so plump and ripe that you wanted to just take a bite out of that beautiful, round peach. I stood there, staring at her for a moment, while the pain in my chest intensified. I knew what she wanted, but I was trying to be a gentleman. I leaned over and moved a stray piece of hair that had fallen over her beautiful face, but she started to stir at my touch, so I quickly pulled my hand back.

"Mmmm...Nico." She was dreaming of *me*, and the last of my restraint snapped. I quickly removed my shoes and socks and threw my shirt next to my jeans. I lay down in just my boxers and spooned her, gently sliding one arm under her head and wrapped the other around her, pulling her flush against my body. She started to move, trying to get comfortable again. Every time she moved, her ass would grind against my cock. After the third time she moved, I wrapped my arm tighter around her so she would quit fucking moving. My dick was hard as stone now.

"Hmmmm...Nico....you...so good...need you." Fuck, there was only so much I could handle, and little Nico wanted to play. I closed my eyes and chanted the spell that would take us both to our dream land.

As soon as I opened my eyes and moved out from behind a tree, I saw her standing there in the clearing. She seemed shocked that she was once again back in her dream land. I waited patiently for her to call out or make any sound. Her long brown hair was loose around her shoulders and flying around her body every time she would spin in a circle, and the white night dress she wore didn't leave much to the imagination.

"Nico! I know this is your doing." She was very perceptive. Not wanting her to wait any longer, I slowly made my way over to her. As soon as her eyes landed on me, they started to travel down my naked chest. I could smell her desire from here. I stopped just a foot in front of her. She craned her neck back so she could look me in the eye.

"Hello, love."

"Why are we here, Nico?" I couldn't admit my own weakness so I focused on hers.

"Because you are not ready for me in the real world, but here I can tend to your needs." I saw the blush start at the base of her neck and make its way all the way to her cheeks. My little vixen was embarrassed.

"Things have changed. We can't do this anymore. You're real and it would complicate things. I mean...You...I...we...can't...." Not wanting to give her a chance to talk herself out of this, I closed the space between us and gripped the back of her head, tugging her hair so I could angle her face perfectly.

She released a breathy moan and that was it. I smashed my lips to hers and began pushing my way into her mouth. She didn't fight me; she opened like she always had for me. She tasted like the sweetest, most addictive drug in the world. I released her hair and pulled back, and the small pout on her face made me smile. Don't worry, love, I am nowhere near done with you.

"Why did you stop?"

"I need to make sure that you're okay with this, love." I didn't want her to wake up tomorrow and hate me for this; I came to her room to tell her something important, but then my other head took over and now here we are, me wanting to fuck her seven ways to Sunday. She dropped her eyes from mine and nibbled on her lip for a moment. I thought she was about to back out, but instead she surprised me by standing on her tiptoes and wrapping her arms around my neck.

"I want this, Nico." I had to make something perfectly clear before we continued, though.

"I will give you whatever you want, love, but on one condition." She groaned.

"What is it?" I slid my arms down her body and placed my

hands on her ass and squeezed, and she gasped. I lifted her off the ground and she wrapped her legs around my waist.

"You never let Kai back into your dreams, only me."

She didn't respond straight away and almost looked like she was about to protest, so I distracted her. I started nibbling on her ear and kissing my way down her neck. Her head lolled back and gave me better access, so I made teasing bites down her collarbone and started sucking on the top of her breast. She was moaning now.

"I need you to answer me, love." I continued to tease her, laying her on the grass and positioning myself between her thighs. I sat back on my heels, running my hands up her parted thighs, stopping before I could push her dress up further.

She wanted me to push her dress up to reveal her most intimate part, but I wouldn't give into her until she gave me what I wanted. I leaned forward and pushed the straps of her dress down so I could expose her tits. They are big and full, her nipples pebbled and ready for my sucking. I didn't make her wait. I lowered my head and began to suck, hard, just how she liked it. She cried out, wanting more, so I used my hand to pinch and twist her other nipple, eliciting another cry from her.

"Nico, please, I need you." This is exactly where I wanted her, begging and ready to give me whatever I wanted. I released her nipple with a pop.

"Agree to my terms, love, and I'll make you come so hard you will be screaming my fucking name!" This time she didn't hesitate.

"I swear, I promise...only you...no Kai. Now fucking make me come!" She didn't have to ask me twice. I kissed my way down her body, pulling her dress with me. Once I reached her hips, she lifted her ass so I could pull her dress off. I chucked it to the side and stared at her sweet glistening pussy. Fuck, I love her cunt.

She was always so wet and ready for me. I used one finger to run through her slick folds and started to rub her clit. She arched her back off the ground and started to moan.

With a smile, I withdrew my hand and positioned myself between her glistening thighs. I opened her with one hand and blew on her enlarged nub; she was squirming and getting agitated. I loved working her to the point where she was begging for me. I leaned forward and ran my tongue from her opening to her clit, pulling a deep moan from her. Stopping at her clit, I began to suck and lick that hard little jewel.

"Nico, more I....need." I pulled back and looked directly into her eyes.

"I know, love." I returned to my task and began eating her sweet pussy again, slipping first one finger and then another in her channel then pumping in and out of her tight sheath. I kept at a fast and hard pace while sucking her clit into my mouth, and before long she was a writhing mess beneath me. I could feel she was close; her walls were gripping my fingers, coaxing me for more.

"Come for me, love." I sucked her clit back into my mouth as she let out a loud cry, screaming my name. The sound of it nearly brought me to completion by itself.

Letting her come down slowly from her high, I withdrew my soaked fingers and traced patterns with them on her soft thighs while I made my way up her body so I could kiss her before I fucked her into oblivion.

CHAPTER 15

Ryan

Oh my God! I felt like I was floating on a cloud. Nico made me come so hard, and fuck did it feel good. He nestled himself between my legs and leaned down to capture my lips in a searing kiss that felt like he was branding me. I could taste myself on his tongue, and I'm not shy to admit that I loved the taste of me mixed with the taste of him. I felt his hard bulge nudging my pussy as he was grinding his pelvis into me. I needed him inside me now.

"Nico, I need you inside me now, please" The smug bastard loved it when I begged.

"You want me to put my cock in this beautiful wet pussy, love?" I loved his dirty talk, it always made me more needy and wet.

"Yes!" It was the only reply he needed before he was stripping himself of his jeans and lining the head of his cock at my entrance. I lifted my head so I could get a better view.

His cock was beautiful, thick and velvety smooth. I know a lot of people think cocks are ugly, but not Nico's; it was a glorious sight to see. I started biting my lip in anticipation, knowing that soon enough he would have me soaring through another orgasm, screaming his name. He ran the tip of his cock from my opening to my clit, bumping slightly against the sensitive nub, making me moan. He kept rubbing the tip of his cock up and down, making me more wild for him. I was about to start begging when he lined himself up with my entrance, looked me in the eye, and slammed into me. The sudden pleasure forced a cry from my lips. I felt so full and complete having him inside me. I felt whole.

"You like that, love?"

"Fuck yes! Fuck me Nico" He was slowly pumping into me and driving me insane; I needed him to fuck me hard and deep, just how I liked it.

"Ask me nicely."

"Please, Nico, fuck me hard so I can come again." With the magic word, he began to slam into my body over and over again. I felt so full, every muscle was strung tight with need. I was close to coming, again.

"Nico, don't stop, please! I'm so close." He never eased his pace, if anything his pace quickened.

"I am going to destroy this pussy, love. You are mine and so is this cunt." As usual, his dirty words were my undoing, and I shattered beneath him, screaming his name.

"Tell me you're mine, tell me this pussy is mine!" I couldn't think straight, and I was still seeing stars. "Tell me now or I won't make you come again, and you can suck my cock instead."

"I'm yours, my pussy is yours. Just yours, Nico, now make me fucking come again, please." He made me come again before he finally found his release, roaring my name. He collapsed on top of me, keeping his full weight from crushing me by resting most of it on his forearms on either side of my head. We lay panting, looking into each other's eyes. I lifted my head and kissed him like my life was depending on it. I was done lying to myself. I was in love with Nicholas Stone and had been for years, even before I knew he was real.

Nico broke our kiss and rolled over, taking me with him, my head resting on his chest. He wrapped both his arms around me, tracing patterns on my bare back. I did the same on his chest, drawing small circles with my fingers. We stayed like that for a long time, neither of us talking, just both enjoying each other's company and embrace.

As I lay there listening to his breathing and the beat of his heart beneath my ear, I started to wonder if we could make this whole marriage thing work. I knew that I loved Nico, and I know a part of him must at least care about me. Together, we could be strong, and in this moment I had no doubt Nico would help me control my powers and wouldn't let me get hurt when we did unlock them.

All the fear I had about my powers disappeared in this moment; I knew I could do this if Nico was by my side. I didn't know how to tell him, so I would show him instead. I pushed away from him and sat up, I saw a look of hurt and confusion on his face—he thought I was trying to leave. No, big man, I plan to show you with my body what you mean to me. He must have read the look on my face, because he relaxed and dropped his head back down. I threw my leg over him so I was now straddling him, and felt his cock come alive beneath me. I couldn't hide my smile. I loved that I had this effect on him.

"Do you plan to ride my cock or sit on it and tease me, love?" His words sent a rush of liquid to my core. I could feel how wet my pussy was. I decided to tease him a bit and started to rub my wet pussy up and down his cock, feeling it harden beneath me. He was ready for me, but I wasn't done playing with him yet.

"Either stick my cock in that beautiful pussy or suck it," he growled, and I shivered at his words. God, it was such a fucking turn on hearing him speak to me like this.

"This time I'm in charge, big man. I get to fuck you how I want." His eyes widened and started to glow a deep purple. I have never taken control like this in my dreams before; Nico was always the one calling the shots.

I could tell my words had shocked him as he kept opening and closing his mouth, not sure what to say. After another minute of rubbing my wet pussy on his cock, I slid down his body and settled myself between his muscular calves.

His eyes lit with fire. He knew what was about to happen. He pushed forward and leaned back on his elbows so he could watch the show. I bent forward and licked the tip of his cock, tasting, teasing. He groaned loudly, and that was all the encouragement I needed. I wrapped my lips around the tip of his cock and began to suck him into my mouth. He was too big to take all the way in, so I used my hand to stroke the base while I sucked and licked the top half.

"Fuuuuccccckkkk, that feels so good, baby. Yeah, just like that." I kept sucking and pumping him into my mouth, and I could taste his pre-cum and still a bit of me on him. It was delicious. "Baby, your mouth feels like fucking heaven, but I need to be inside you now!" He didn't have to ask me twice, I released his cock with a pop and straddled his hips, lining his cock up with my opening.

I wanted this hard and fast, so I slammed myself down onto his shaft, both of us crying out at the same time. I began to rock my hips. He felt so much deeper with me being on top. Within just a few moments I was close already, my pussy was pulsing and he was thrusting upward every time I moved back, hitting just the right spot. God, I wouldn't last much longer.

"Nico, I'm coming!" As soon as the words were out of my mouth, I tipped over the edge, and he took over, wrapping both his arms around my waist and pounding his cock inside me. I was screaming his name to the heavens. In one swift move he had me pinned on my back and he was on top, back in control.

"That was fucking hot, baby but now it's my turn, and I'm

out of patience." My only response was to moan; I was spent. That last orgasm took it out of me. True to his word, Nico fucked me hard and fast and ripped another orgasm from me. Once he reached his peak, he collapsed to the side of me and pulled me into his arms. I couldn't keep my eyes open any longer...I was bone tired after so many orgasms.

I must have drifted off, because next thing I knew, I woke to Nico's face between my legs, eating my pussy. He made me come all over his face and then fucked me senseless. He woke me two more times after that, taking me from the back the first time, and then the last time was very different.

I woke to him scattering kisses all over my tired, naked body. He had positioned himself between my legs and then kissed me. This kiss felt different—there was so much emotion behind it that it stole my breath. He wasn't fucking me this time, he was...he was making love to me. Nico and I had never done the whole slow, make love thing...we liked to go hard, deep and fast. He broke the kiss and pulled back so he could look me in the eyes as he was slowly working his way in and out of my body.

"You are everything to me, my love. You are the sun on my darkest days and the light on my darkest nights. You, my love, are my queen." I couldn't hold my tears back. They started rolling down my face, but he didn't say anything or stop moving inside me, instead just leaning down and licking and kissing away my tears, murmuring how much he loved my body and how beautiful I was.

His thrusts started to pick up speed, and I wrapped my legs around his hips and pulled down, pressing him deeper inside me.

"What do you need love?"

"I need you deeper and harder, Nico, please." He gave me more of his weight as he picked up speed and began punishing me with his hard thrusts. It was so right.

"Don't stop, please!" And he didn't stop, until we were both screaming our release. I felt so sated and relaxed. As soon as Nico pulled out of me, I felt his essence leaking down my thighs, and he watched as his cum slid out of me with a satisfied smile on his face. Once more he lay down beside me and gathered me in his arms. I was drifting off to sleep when I heard him whisper.

"Please forgive me when you learn what I have done. I cannot lose you, baby. You are my hugacko." I tipped into the darkness before I could respond, and slept soundly for the first time in weeks.

CHAPTER 16

Nico

As soon as she drifted off to sleep, I chanted the spell to bring us back to her bedroom in Jackson's compound. The sun was already rising, and I knew sleep would evade me. I had never felt like this for anyone in my many years of being alive. I laid there, just looking at her sleep in my arms. Her tiny body was nestled in the same position as it was before I took her to our dreamland, and I ran my hand up and down her side, just needing to feel her. As soon as she learned the truth about what I had done she would hate me. I am the reason she is here. I don't have the balls to tell her the truth, but I know I need to find a way before Kai tells her. I lay there watching her sleep for so long that I must have drifted off too, jerked awake sometime later by a constant knocking on her door. Before I could untangle myself, the door smashed open and slammed against the wall. Ryan sat straight up, ready to scream, until she saw it was Kai, Dom, and Jax in the doorway, I didn't bother to move off the bed; I just sat up and wrapped my arms around her waist and rested my chin on her shoulder, glaring at the three bastards who disturbed us.

"I have a key, dumb ass, there was no need to break my

fucking door." Jax was clearly pissed that Kai was busting up the place.

"You weren't fast enough," Kai snapped at him.

"Both of you shut up. Clearly she's fine, judging by the way she won't make eye contact with us and is blushing so hard you would think she was sunburnt. I think she had a great night's rest, aye love?" I couldn't hide my smile.

Instead of answering Dom, I placed a kiss on Ryan's cheek, which caused her to blush even more. I loved watching her blush.

"How about we give you guys twenty minutes and then you meet us in the mess hall? We need to finalize these wedding plans." With that reality check from Dom, I unwrapped my arms from around Ryan and stood. I stopped moving and turned toward Dom when he whistled. I realized then that I was only in my boxers. Ryan turned her head and looked at me, her mouth was hanging open so I leaned over and used a finger to close it for her.

"You're drooling, baby," I said with a wink. She shook her head and snapped herself out of it.

"You slept in here with me, like that?" I laughed, after everything that happened last night in our dream, she was worried that I slept next to her in boxers.

"Baby, if I recall, I spent more time naked and inside you than I did in these." She blushed a dark shade of red and dropped her eyes. My little sex devil was shy in the light of day.

"You fucked her?" I snapped my gaze to Melakai, who was shaking with anger. Dom and Jax were holding him back. Ryan flinched at Kai's outburst, which made me furious. She had nothing to feel guilty about.

"Kai, I..." I cut Ryan's reply off, we didn't need to explain ourselves to him. We were about to be married!

"That is none of your fucking business. She is about to be

my wife, and what we do and don't do in the confines of our bedchamber is not your concern. Oh, and from now on, you will stay the fuck out of her dreams." I heard Ryan gasp, and she turned her angry glare my way.

"You do not get to tell me what to do, Nico!"

"Actually, love, yeah, I do. You promised me!" She was seething now, I could see the fire in her eyes, and damn that look alone was starting to wake my cock.

"You can't fucking hold that against me! Of course I would say whatever the hell you wanted when you wouldn't let me FUCKING COME!" As soon as the words flew out of her mouth, she slapped a hand over her lips and quickly looked back to where the three guys were standing in the doorway, looking varying degrees of shocked and furious. Ryan quickly dropped her head and stared at her lap; even I was shocked at her outburst. I never expected that to come out of her mouth, no pun intended.

"So, yeah, we're just like gonna go to the hall mess. I mean mess hall. And wait for you guys to come. I mean get there." I wanted to laugh at Dom, I had never seen him so out of sorts. All three men quickly left, even Melakai didn't make a fuss as he was ushered out of the room by Dom. Jax closed what was left of the door, and I made a mental note to make sure he got that fixed by this evening.

"Please don't say a word, Nico, just go and I will meet you at the mess hall." She flopped back on the bed and pulled the covers over her face. I couldn't leave her like this. She was so adorable when she was shy and embarrassed. I jumped back on the bed and ripped the covers away from her. Before she could protest, I hopped on top of her and wrestled my way between her legs. She tried to fight me, but she knew she would lose. With a groan, she opened them for me and I settled there. I leaned down so I could kiss her cheek, then her neck, and eventually found my way to her mouth. I thought she might turn away or try pushing me off, but she didn't, opening for me as soon as I prodded her mouth with my tongue. She tasted so sweet; I wanted to stay here and do this all day and hopefully bury my dick inside of her while we were both awake. But I knew if we both didn't get our asses up and to the mess hall, the whole gang would come to us. I pulled back and smiled down at her, and to my surprise, she didn't blush. I saw the desire burning in her eyes. With a groan, I quickly jumped off the bed and told her I would be back after a quick shower to get her, and she should get ready before the others came back.

After a quick shower and shave, I made my way back to Ryan's room to collect her. Just as I rounded the last bend, I saw two guys at her door already pulling the old door off and had a new one leaning against the wall. As soon as she saw me, she made her way out of her room and stood in front of me, chewing her bottom lip. I reached out and tugged her lip so she would stop chewing it; at the rate she was going she would chew the damn thing off.

"Sorry, nervous gesture, I always seem to do that or pace."

"Nothing to be nervous about, love, and by the way, you look beautiful." She blushed at my compliment; she was wearing skin-tight black jeans and a snug white V-neck shirt. That reminded me— she was wearing Aurora's clothes. I would organize Larick to go back and retrieve her and her cousins' belongings. I also needed to give her the letter from her father that she didn't know I had.

"Thank you." She grasped my hand and began to pull me along, and when I finally snapped out of my shock, I took control and took the lead. She laughed, knowing that I was always the one that had to be in control. I may have let her have her moment last night, but not today. We made it to the mess hall in record time, and both of us had smiles on our faces as we entered. As we walked past the buffet, I saw her tense and drop her head. I strained my hearing and then I heard the whispers.

"Isn't she the Alpha's mate?"

"I thought she was fucking the Day-walker."

"Eww look at her, next thing you know she will be fucking the half-breed." I turned to put an end to this gossip when she stopped me with a hand on my arm.

"Don't, Nico. Let them think what they want. You jumping to my defense only makes it worse." At her request I let it go, but as we made our way through the tables to head toward the guys, the whispers intensified. There was one woman bold enough to even shout out her insult, which had Ryan freezing in her tracks and me glaring over her head at the woman.

"You're the Alpha's mate, but you fuck a leech and the king of the fae. You are trash! I don't know what they see in you." I waited for Ryan to drop her head or cry or something, but she shocked me when she replied to the bitch.

"They see a woman who can handle three alpha males all at once. Jealousy will get you nowhere, sweetheart." I turned to see the guys at our table with their mouths hanging open in shock; even my sister and Aurora looked taken back by Ryan's reply.

"You're a vile, disgusting bitch."

"And you're a jealous whore, but you don't see me standing here complaining about it, do you? Just so were clear, sweetheart, who I fuck is none of your concern." With that said, she made her way over to our table with her head held high. I felt like a dog following its master. I was so turned on by the way she finally stood up for herself. When we made it to our table, everyone was still staring at her.

"Close your mouth, Dom, you'll catch flies." Dom quickly shut his mouth then opened it. I wasn't sure which was worse.

"You are amazing! Marry me, not that good-for-nothing king." I was so close to punching Dom in the face and I hadn't even had breakfast.

"I guess I could add you to my *apparent* harem." Aurora and Sophia burst into laughter. I, on the other hand, was pissed. No way in hell would any of these guys be going near her. It was bad enough that fucking Kai has already been with her. She took a seat between Aurora and Chase and began to eat her breakfast. I was still standing, glaring at her. When she looked up and our eyes connected, she frowned.

"What's your problem big guy? Your mood swings are giving me whiplash." I could hear Jax and Dom snickering and that fucked me off more.

"He's just pissy because you said you wanted to add me to your harem." Fucking Dominic!

She just rolled her eyes and joined in on the conversation her cousins were having about our upcoming marriage. I begrudgingly took the last seat available, which just happened to be next to Kai, lucky me. He shot me a glare when I sat down, and his behavior didn't go unnoticed by Ryan.

"Why do you both look like you're about two seconds away from throwing hands?" Neither of us responded to her questions as Aurora began to shake next to her. The only time

Aurora really touches anyone is when she is viewing their past; other than that, she avoids contact as much as possible.

A hush falls over the mess hall as everyone waits and watches Aurora. She is revered for her visions. She has saved this pack more times than any wolf shifter. Her visions allow Jackson to see any threat before it happens. After a couple of minutes, Aurora slumps forward and catches herself on the table. She's panting hard and fast. Jax quickly jumps from his seat and makes his way over to her, handing her a glass of water.

"It's okay, you're okay. Deep breaths, babe." Even now Jackson doesn't touch her, he just reassures her with his words. "Take your time." After another few moments, Aurora's gaze turns to me and I gulp—this can't be good.

"You have the letter?" *How the fuck*...of course she knows I took the letter Ryan's dad wrote her. Reluctantly, I nod.

"What letter?" Fucking Dom. I swear I am going to stitch his mouth shut. I wait for Aurora to answer, knowing Ryan is going to go off.

"The letter Ryan's father wrote her; she needs to read it." Before Ryan or anyone can answer or yell at me for having the letter, I ask,

"Why?"

"Because it will help Ryan understand what happened to her sister."

"What do you mean?" Ryan's concern is evident in her voice.

"Read the letter now, you have until sundown to figure it out."

"What happens at sundown, Rora?" Chase asks the question that is on everyone's mind.

"Stevie Knox will arrive here at sundown, at the northern border, to see her sister." You can hear Ryan's sharp intake of breath and both her cousins gasp.

"She will not breach our borders! I will—" Aurora cuts Jax off before he can finish.

"You will let her through! She will not harm Ryan. Nico, you need to be ready. She is coming to speak to her sister, but she is coming for your blood!" *Fuck me.* What is it with these Knox women and wanting to kill me?

CHAPTER 17

Ryan

Stevie's coming, Nico hid something from me *again*, and Stevie wants to kill Nico. I keep running those words through my head on a loop. What did Nico do? Why would Stevie be coming here? Has she had a change of heart? Oh my God, Kai will have to face her. I didn't even think of Kai. As soon as Aurora finished telling us her vision, I left the mess hall and returned to my room, needing some time to sort my head out and prepare for my sister's arrival. Now I had to read the letter from my dad that Nico somehow has. Why does he keep breaking my fucking trust? Speak of the devil. The man himself has just walked through my bedroom door, without knocking.

"When a door is shut it means you need to knock!"

"I didn't knock last night, and it seemed to work out well for the both of us." The fucking *cheek* of this arrogant asshole!

"I was asleep, Nico!"

"Still, you can't tell me you didn't enjoy that dream." He was teasing me, and I was about ready to skin him alive.

"What do you want?" At my question, the carefree look on his face dropped, and he reached into the back pocket of his jeans and pulled out the letter from my dad. I didn't move, I just stood there staring at him. After a beat, he sighed and closed the distance between us. He lifted my limp arm and placed the letter in my hand. I wasn't ready to read this, but now I was out of time and had no choice. After a moment, I closed my fingers around the letter and pulled my arm from his grasp. He turned to leave but stopped when there was a knock at the door.

"Come in," he said.

"This isn't your fucking room—" I stopped talking as soon as I saw Larkin enter, carrying my suitcase and duffel bag that I left behind at the cabin we were staying in when we first got to Alaska. "How did you get those?" Larkin didn't answer, he simply deposited my bags by the foot of the bed and left the room, closing the door behind him.

"I sent Larkin to retrieve them this morning; I thought you might like your belongings back. I also got him and Maverick to retrieve your cousins' belongings. You should also know that the cabin is empty. Your sister isn't staying there." Where the hell was Stevie staying, then? Nico turned to leave, but I stopped him.

"Thank you for getting our stuff, but I need to know two things, Nico." He stiffened but wouldn't turn to face me. After a long sigh, he responded.

"Ask away, little one."

"How did you get the letter my dad wrote?"

"I snuck into your room one night at the cabin and took it, in case it held information that your sister could use against us." That was...that was actually smart.

"Did you read it?"

"No, now ask what you really want to know, love."

"Why is my sister coming after you?"

"She thinks I killed your father." See, I thought that at the start, when Aurora told us, but now I think it's something else.

"I don't believe you."

He didn't answer, just shook his head and left the room. After hearing the door click shut, I quickly made my way over to the door and locked it. I know it was dumb to think a lock would stop him from getting in, but it made me feel more secure. With a few deep breaths, I walked over to the single chair by the window and sat down. It was time to woman up and read this damn letter. I sent up a silent prayer to my dad, asking him to help me make sense of this whole shit show that has become my life. With another deep breath, I ripped the envelope open and pulled out the letter that was actually two pages. Seeing my dad's handwriting brought tears to my eyes. I knew reading this letter was going to hurt and open up old wounds of never having my father in my life. After a few more deep breaths, I began to read the letter.

To my dearest Ry,

If you are reading this, it means I am no longer alive. I would have given anything to have you in my arms one last time or just to be able to tell you that I love you. You are so special, Ryan. You are more than I could have ever hoped for.

I may not have been able to see you or protect you from

the horrors you have lived through, but believe me, my dear, I know all about them.

The woman you live with now is not the woman I married.

You having this letter means Stevie has told you about what you are, but your sister doesn't know the full story. Stevie will take you to our coven in Wonder Lake, and you will learn about your gifts. I need you to find a man named Jackson Marshall. He is the Alpha of the Alaskan Wolf pack, and he has a seer within his pack that will help you. The seer will tell you everything else you need to know. She will tell you where to find a man named Nicholas Stone; he is the king of the fae and a good friend of mine. He is the key to help you unlock your gifts.

Once you have done all this, there is something else you need to know, daughter. I have done something that you will not be happy about. You have powers that are beyond this world. I didn't know about your gifts till it was too late, and I am sorry that I have failed you, my dear.

In order for you to survive the release of your powers, you need to wed a man from another realm. When two worlds merge as one, you will be released from the confines of the block he placed on you.

I had to change the original spell the king performed so he could never use you without your consent. You must agree and want to wed in order for my spell to break. I added this failsafe in case of my death, so you would have to be willing and not forced. It was the only way I could protect you without someone trying to use you for your gifts.

I am so sorry for all of this. I wish I was there to guide you, my dear girl. You are stronger than any other supernatural; your power is what can lock the fae realm, not your blood, like the legend has foretold. Your blood is the key, though, to grant vampires the ability to walk in the daylight. I know this must be a lot to take in, but I have more to say yet.

The day I turned you away, when you came to the house, I had no other choice! Your sister is changing, and the day you came was one of her bad days. You see, the legend left out the part that one twin would be born pure of heart and good, while the other would be born of darkness.

Your sister is losing control faster than I could have imagined; this darkness inside her needs to lead and craves power and destruction. She wants me to step down and let her lead the Knox coven, but I can't have that. She is not the true heir to the throne, you are! She will try to take the throne from you, Ryan, and you cannot let that happen. You need to go to the Knox coven and find a lady named Mya, she will help you, and you can trust her.

You need to save your sister! She needs you. Once you learn to control the power you wield, you can banish the darkness inside her. This will come at a cost, but I *haven't been able to find out what that cost is. Mya may have been able to find this out in my absence. Your mother was also cursed, my dear; her mother's spell backfired. She thought she cast a spell that would conceal the child from anyone who wished to harm her—that wasn't the case. She messed up somehow, and your mother paid the price for your grandmother's mistake. Mya can tell you this story when you find her.*

Your sister has just arrived home, so I need to go now, my dear. Just remember that you are strong and you are worthy. You can do this, daughter. I know you can, as my blood runs in your veins. I love you to infinity and beyond Ry-Ry.

Love always and forever,

Dad xx

I burst out into uncontrollable sobs, my heart breaking and begging for my dad. He fucking loved me, and that bitch kept me away from him. I hated my mother more than I ever had in this moment. I felt the power inside of me building and heating my blood. I didn't try to stop it or calm down; I needed to release the pain inside of me. I screamed out, and as I did, a blast of blue light shot out from inside me. I slumped back into my chair, sobbing. When I felt two strong arms wrap around me, I didn't scream or flinch. At this point, whoever it was could kill me and it would hurt less than the pain in my chest. I was lifted from the chair and then cradled in someone's lap; my eyes may have been open, but they were so cloudy from all the tears rushing from them that I still couldn't see.

"I got you, love. You're okay." Dom was the one holding me and stroking my hair while I broke apart in front of him. I didn't feel embarrassed or ashamed, just numb and shattered. "Let it all out, babe. I promise I'll hold you through it all." His kind words made me cry harder. I cried for the loss of my dad, the loss of the life I could have had, and the loss of my sister to this darkness that was eating her alive.

"I....I...I....didn't...say...bye." I couldn't form a proper sentence; I was hiccupping and sobbing too much.

"You didn't say bye to who, love?"

"D...D....Dad." I cried harder, the guilt was killing me. I never said goodbye to my dad, I never went to his funeral. I was too angry at him, because I thought he abandoned me.

I thought he chose my sister over me. He thought I would be safe with my mother, so he took the child that he thought needed his help more. I turned in Dom's lap so I was pretty much straddling him and wrapped my arms around his neck and buried my face in the crook of his neck. He didn't say anything, just moved my legs so they were on the outside of his thighs; he used one hand to stroke my hair and the other to rub up and down my back. I don't know how long we stayed like that, but it must have been a while, because I dozed off and woke to the sound of voices.

"Now is not the time for this fucking conversation and your jealousy, Nicky boy." I smiled internally at Dom calling Nico *Nicky boy.* "She needed me to hold her while she broke; she is hurt and angry. You need to start telling her the fucking truth. I will not sit by any longer and watch this beautiful girl be destroyed by you." Dom was sticking up for me, a notion that had my heart warming.

"She is not yours to hold! She is mine. What is it with you

three and constantly telling me how to deal with her? Stay the fuck out of my business, Dominic."

"Fuck you, Nicky boy. If she wanted you here, she would say it, but she isn't, is she? We know you're awake, love, and if you want me to swap with Nico I will, if not I'll kick the bastard out." I didn't lift my head or say a word, just shook my head. "Well, there you have it, Nico. Get out and send someone to fix her door again. I broke it down getting in here to her." The room was silent for a moment, all you could hear was loud breathing and I am assuming *that* noise was coming from Nico.

"Fuck. Fucking fuck. Ryan, I'll be outside waiting." I didn't acknowledge Nico's words, just remained buried in the crook of Dom's neck. "Just know that I am sorry and that I am here if you need me." I heard the sound of footsteps and then the door squeaking shut.

"He's gone now, babe." I slowly started to untangle my arms from around his neck and lean back, so I could look at him. I expected to see pity in his eyes, but all I saw was understanding. That shocked me. How could he possibly understand what I am going through?

"Do you want to talk about it?" I sat and pondered his request, my eyes skipping to the door that is just hanging on by the hinges at an odd angle. Dom understands what I am saying without words. "I cast a spell as soon as he stepped out; he can't hear us." Wow, Dom really was a powerful warlock. I didn't even hear him utter any words. I made a move to get off Dom's lap, feeling awkward for the position we were in. His arms shot out and locked around my waist; I snapped my eyes to him in confusion. "How about I take you to your favorite place and we can chat there?"

"Okay," is my only reply, Dom helps me from his lap. My legs feel numb from being crammed into the chair for so long. Dom bends down and retrieves the letter from my dad. I don't say a word as he folds the note up and puts it back into the envelope.

He hands me the letter, and I quickly shove it into my back pocket, not wanting to see my dad's handwriting again. Dom turns away from me and starts to chant.

I guess he's opening a portal to Lake William. Once the portal is open and Lake William is visible on the other side, Dom grasps my hand in his and starts to lead me toward the portal. Just before we enter, I hear loud noises coming from outside.

"Dominic! Un-bar this fucking door now! I can feel your power and know you have opened a portal." Dom starts laughing. I look to him, confused as fuck.

"I also spelled the door so no one else could break in." I smile at his deviousness. *What a bloody clever warlock you are, Dom.* "Hang on, I need to remove the sound spell." Dom says a few words under his breath that I don't understand and then shouts, "Be back soon, Nicky boy, we have three hours to kill before the wicked witch gets here." With that said, he grabs my hand again and we step through the portal.

Lake William is beautiful, surrounded by mountains and trees as far as the eye can see. The old jetty sways as the wind blows the lake's water. I make my way down the pier and sit, Dom joins me and dangles his feet over the edge as well. We don't speak for a while, just stare out at the beauty that is Lake William. This place has brought me so much happiness over the years; I can't explain, but I feel like this place is a part of me.

"You know Nico is probably going to beat my ass when we get back." Shocked, I turn and look at Dom to see if he's joking, but he's not.

"Why?"

"Because Nico isn't the only one who can hide his tracks. When a portal opens, it leaves a magic signature behind, just like every magic user has a different signature." I nod my head, not really sure where he is going with this. "Well, I made sure that my portal left a trail to follow to South America." At his admission we both start laughing knowing Nico would be furious and trying to find us.

"He doesn't scare me."

"I know he doesn't love, sometimes he wishes you were afraid of him so you wouldn't keep running from him."

"I will never fear him, I only run because..."

"You run because you're feeling more than you want to for the angry bastard, and *that* scares you." Well, fuck me with a silver spoon, Dom was more intuitive than I gave him credit for.

CHAPTER 18

Ryan

I avert my eyes from Dom's face so he can't see the truth; the truth is Dom is right. I am scared of what I am feeling for Nico.

"Take it from someone who has been where you are, babe—don't run, embrace it."

"How have you been where I am?" I sound like a bitch, but come on. Look at Dom; what stupid woman would run from him? He's beautiful, with those violet eyes, sun-kissed skin and shaggy silver-blond hair that you wanted to run your hands through. He was a handsome man, but he was also kind and caring. He would give you the shirt off his back if you needed it.

"I was in a similar situation many years ago, and I was too much of a coward to admit my feelings. I lost my chance with the one I crave, but you haven't lost Nico, there is hope for you two. I see the way my friend looks at you, and I see the way you look at him. You are both stubborn fuckers, and sooner or later one of you has to give in."

"Who broke your heart?" What can I say, when in doubt, deflect the attention to someone else.

"I know what you're trying to do and it won't work. We're

here to talk about you, not me." Well, there goes that plane of deflecting the attention from me and my fucked-up love life.

"I don't want to talk about me, though. I swear I'm not really that interesting"

"I beg to differ, love, you are an anomaly, and have been fated to marry my best friend but loved my other best friend, and then he died and now he's back and now you don't want to jump his bones." Well, when he put it like that, I sounded like a fucking hussy.

"I don't want to talk about Kai."

"Okay, how about you tell me why you are so upset, reading a letter from your father, but you're fine when you have daydreams about him?" Okay I guess we were getting into the heavy shit.

"How do you know about me seeing my dad?"

"I may have done a little spell so I could listen in on you and Nico the other day when you were here." Fucking wanker! He heard me confess everything to Nico, and now he wanted to sit there with a fucking smug look on his face.

"You fucking bastard, how dare you—"

"I did it in case Nico lost his cool and I needed to step in. I never meant to hear all of that, I swear. I would never have done it if I didn't worry Nico would go ape shit. I didn't hear everything, I stopped listening after that."

"Why would he go ape shit?" Dom turned and looked out over the lake for a moment. I waited patiently knowing he would eventually tell me when he was ready.

"Nico is jealous and overprotective of you because you are his *hugacko*."

"What is a hugacko?"

"Werewolves have mates, as you know. Their soulmate, if you will. Werewolves, after they turn, can scent out a mate. They will travel the world to pick up on the scent of their mate.

Well, for a fae, it is much more complex. There is no scent to follow; they physically have to be in the presence of the person to find their hugacko. The last time a fae found their hugacko was over a hundred years ago."

"Why didn't Nico tell me?"

"Because when a fae finds their other half, normally they understand the feeling and accept the bond straightaway. Your fae half hasn't been unlocked yet, so he is hoping that when it is unlocked, you will feel the bond as he does."

"That doesn't answer my question, Dom." I could tell he didn't want to answer me but we have gone too far into this conversation for him to pull back now.

"Nico didn't want this discovery to have any sway over your decision to marry him. He wanted you to marry him because you have feelings for him and not out of duty to a bond you don't even know about."

I sat there, stunned for a long while, mulling over what Dom had just said. Nico is an asshole most of the time, but him keeping this from me isn't his normal asshole behavior. Him keeping this from me is one of the sweetest things he could have done. He didn't want to pressure me.

"What if I flat out refused to marry him and say to hell with the fae realm?" Dom laughed.

"He would have tried fucking hard to convince you to change your mind. Nico is a controlling prick and expects people to yield to him, but when it comes to you he's different."

"How so?"

"He would have let the love of his life—his soul mate—leave him and his people to die, if that is what you really wanted. He would never force you to stay, Ryan, even if it broke him to let you leave." This new discovery about Nico was doing weird things to my heart. I cared about Nico so much. I didn't want to lose him, but I still couldn't trust him. He has lied to me so many times.

"How about a change of subject?" It hit me that Dom could help me find Mya.

"I need your help."

"I have a feeling helping you with this task is going to get my ass kicked by the broody bastard who's trying to track our whereabouts." I giggled at Dom's description of Nico. He wasn't wrong; Nico really was a broody bastard.

"I need you to help me find someone." Dom turned and stared at me, like he was trying to decipher my deepest secrets.

"Who and why?" Here goes. I need to be honest with him. I owe him that much if he is going to help me.

"A lady named Mya; she is from the Knox coven. She is the lady that can hopefully help me save my sister." The look Dom gave me told me how skeptical he was—he didn't think my sister was savable. I wasn't sure, myself.

CHAPTER 19

Nico

"I'm going to kill that fucking bastard!"

"Calm down, Nico, you know he will keep her safe." I turned to pin Jackson with a fucking death glare. The look I had on my face had him shutting his mouth real quick. That smug fucking bastard masked his trail and sent me on a fucking wild goose chase through South fucking America. I was going to kill him.

"They have been gone for fucking hours!" I was going out of my mind, worrying and wondering if she was safe. What if her sister got to her or even fucking worse what if Randall managed to ambush them?

"Brother, they have only been gone for just under two hours, Dom said he would be back before her sister arrived, correct?" I looked to Sophia, who was occupying the single seat by the window in Ryan's room. I knew she was right. Dom would bring her back before her sister arrived, but it didn't stop me worrying though.

"What if they got ambushed or something?" I voiced my fear to the group. Jax, Kai, Aurora, Sophia, and Ryan's cousins came running when they heard me threatening to kill Dom when I felt him open a portal. Kai and I tried to break the door down, but couldn't break through Dominic's magic. I had to ask her fucking cousins to help me break the seal. I hated how strong Dom's magic was. It hurt my pride so much having to ask those bags of dicks for help. They may be Ryan's cousins but they were annoying assholes.

"Dominic would lay down his life for hers." I pinned Kai with a look that told him out of everyone in this room he was the last person I wanted to answer my question. "Hate me all you want *king*, but I will always protect her and so would Dom. We know what she is to you now." Hearing him admit that he knew Ryan was my hugacko filled me with a sense of relief; he knew he could never have her or take her from me. She was made for me.

I felt the whoosh of a portal opening behind me and spun around to see Dominic walk through with Ryan's hand clasped in his. I saw red, already moving toward him, ready to beat the fucking bastard till he was begging. As soon as I was within striking distance, I cocked my arm back, ready to hit the prick, when Ryan rushed in front of him and screamed at me.

"Stop!" I dropped my arm to my side, glaring over her head at my best friend.

"He has it coming! Now move, love." I was seething and so ready to unleash my pent-up rage on Dominic's face.

"Step aside, babe, I got this." He just fucking called her babe! That was it—he was losing fucking teeth for that. Shaking her head and looking at me, she said.

"I promised Dom I wouldn't let you hurt him. Don't make me break that promise, Nico." The way she was looking at me was like a mother telling her toddler he couldn't have one last cookie before bed.

"I didn't promise shit!" Fuck, now I was starting to sound like a toddler.

"Nico, stop acting like a fucking child and sit your ass down." Fucking Jackson was next on my "beat the shit out of him" list. I growled and made my way over to her bed and sat on the end next to Aurora.

"Where have you two been?" Jax asked, but Melakai answered for Dom and Ryan.

"Lake William, I presume?" Both Dom and Ryan shared a look then nodded.

"How did you know that? I masked my trail so no one could follow us." Fucking Dom turned and winked at me, and I rose from the bed, ready to beat the shit out of him, when Ryan started to shout at us both.

"Nico, sit the hell down now! Dom, stop antagonizing him, you know he's brooding. Don't make the old man have a heart attack before we make it down the aisle." With that they both started fucking laughing. She called me brooding and old! What the actual fuck. Well, two can play at this game, sweetheart.

"My brooding old ass still managed to have you screaming my fucking name last night." She stopped laughing immediately. Everyone was silent, you could of heard a pin drop, it was so fucking quiet in the room.

"Wow, that was a dick move, brother." Dom wrapped his arm around her and whispered something in her ear. I was trying so hard to bite my tongue and not make an even bigger fool of myself. She blew out a long exhale and then turned her hazel eyes to me.

"You need to stop saying shit like that, Nico. This isn't a dick measuring contest. I am pretty sure everyone in this room knows our history. We're about to get married tomorrow, so you don't need to be so overprotective, okay?" I released the breath I didn't know I was holding. She was right; I had to stop lashing out. But this bond between her and I was making me crazy. I needed to have her in my sight at all times just to ease this ache in my chest.

"Look we're running out of time before Stevie arrives. Aurora, do you have any idea what she wants?" Alex asked.

"Only that she wants to speak to Ryan. I'm sorry, Alex, but that is all I could see. Well, that and Ryan needed to read the letter her dad had written her." Shit, I really needed to know what that letter said; seeing how broken she was in Dom's arms earlier nearly broke me. I could tell the letter had some hard truths in it. Ryan clammed up at the mention of the letter, obviously not wanting to discuss it with anyone. That notion burned a little, knowing that she didn't want to share it with me. "Ryan, is there anything you want to tell us." I could feel it in my gut that Aurora saw more in her vision, but she didn't want to betray Ryan's trust.

"Squirt, is there something you want to tell us?" Ryan turned to her cousin and then looked back to Dom; he gave her a curt nod and an encouraging smile. With a loud exhale she turned back to Alex.

"I don't want to go into details, as that letter was something private between my father and I, but there was something in the letter. There is a way we can save my sister, maybe." Alex and Chase exchanged a look of disbelief. I can't blame them; there was no cure for crazy.

"I don't think there is a way to save Stevie from herself, Ry..."

"You're wrong, Chase. *'The legend left out the part that one twin would be born pure of heart and good, while the other would be born of darkness.'* That's what my dad said, if I can learn to control my powers, I can banish the darkness from inside her. I need your guys help, please." Both Alex and Chase reluctantly nodded.

"We'll help you however we can, Ry." She seemed relieved

that Chase and Alex were willing to help her try to save her sister, but I could feel there was more she wasn't telling us.

"I will meet with Stevie today, and while she is distracted with me, Chase, I need you and Alex to go with Dom."

"What? Go where?" Chase took the words right out of my mouth.

"I need you to go with Dom back to the Knox coven and find a lady named Mya." It was clear both her cousins knew who this Mya is. "You know her?"

"Yeah, Ry, everyone knows Mya." Alex cut Chase off then and took over the conversation.

"She was the second in command to your father. She ran the coven while your dad was back in New Zealand. She is very old and wise, and if she went missing, everyone would notice."

"Then ask her nicely to come with you and let her know the true coven queen needs her help." To say I was shocked at my sister's input would be an understatement. Since when did she get so wise?

I really needed to sit down and have a talk with my sister. She was continuing to not only surprise me, but Jax and Dom as well. Kai seemed like he was accustomed to this new Sophia. It pissed me off more that he knew my sister better than I did.

Everyone started making a plan on what was to happen. Ryan would meet Stevie, with Jax and I there, as well. Dom and her cousins would go find this Mya. Kai, Aurora and Sophia would finish the arrangements for the wedding tomorrow.

We needed to make sure Kai stayed out of sight, we couldn't let Stevie get wind of him being alive, yet. I felt for Kai in this moment; Kai always thought we would find a cure for him so he wouldn't be a vampire for all eternity.

He hated that he had to drink the blood of others. Dom and I had searched for years for a potion or a spell or something to return Kai to his fae form. Kai was the first fae to ever be turned into a vampire. We learned from Kai that a fae's blood remains pure in their vampire form; it doesn't dilute and disappear like a witch's or a humans. Because of that, we thought we had a chance to save him. But his fae blood is gone, taken by the spell that brought him back to life.

Ryan, Jax, and I made our way to the boundary gate where Aurora told us Stevie would be. Just before we cleared the edge of the woods to enter the clearing, Jax started growling. That immediately set me on edge, and I reached for Ryan, pulling her behind me.

"What's going on?"

"Your sister isn't alone; she brought the traitor with her!" Oh, that's what Jax could smell. He must have caught the scent of Tyler. I released Ryan's arm and stepped aside. She took a deep breath and straightened to her full height and held her head high. Jax and I walked on either side of her. We weren't trusting of Ryan's sister, so we made sure to have Jax's best wolves stationed around the area in case of an ambush. I wouldn't take any unnecessary risks with Ryan's life. She knew there were wolves stationed in the trees, as we told her the plan before we left the compound, and surprisingly she didn't argue with us.

We walked for a few more minutes and then finally emerged into the clearing. Ryan's step faltered at the sight of her sister but recovered quickly and continued to walk toward her sister. I was so fucking proud of Ryan. She was growing stronger by the day. A few weeks ago she would never have been able to do this. She has grown within herself, and the change was so noticeable now. She walked taller and with more confidence; she spoke her mind and wouldn't let others speak down to her. She was still scared and timid, don't get me wrong, but she hid it better now. She was going to be the greatest queen Farrarie had ever fucking seen. I was one lucky son of a bitch.

CHAPTER 20

Ryan

As soon as we emerged from the woods and into the clearing, I stumbled. Seeing my sister for the first time since everything happened was hard. Stevie had changed, physically. She had cut her hair shorter now, into a pixie cut, and her eyes seemed dull and dark now. Her face had hardened.

Gone was the carefree look she used to have. Stevie wore jeans and a simple black shirt that was cut to show off her midriff. She wore black Chucks on her feet. How the hell was she not freezing? The temperature had dropped significantly. We stopped a few feet from her. I couldn't stop staring at my sister, and she was staring right back. I felt inadequate in her presence; Before we left I had changed and dressed in my own clothes. It felt good to have my own things again. I was wearing black skinny jeans and my favorite Joker and Harley Quinn shirt, which was covered by my thick jacket. I wasn't used to this type of cold; Alaska was kicking my ass. You could smell in the air that it was about to snow. The weather here changed so suddenly; it was warm and sunny yesterday, and today it was freaking cold.

It was starting to get awkward, just standing here between

Jax and Nico while staring at my sister and Tyler. Tyler seemed like he wanted to be anywhere but here, and I found that strange. He betrayed his pack and his sister to help *my* sister and Randall. Why would he do that? I cocked my head to the side, staring at him, trying to figure out what his motive was for betraying his friends and family. Tyler started to squirm under the pressure of my gaze.

"Stop staring at me like that!" Tyler clearly didn't like having the attention on him, which urged me to continue. He started shuffling from foot to foot.

"Why are you doing this, Tyler?" The question flew out of my mouth before I could stop it. I couldn't let him or my sister see that I rattled my own cage by having no control over my vocal cords; Stevie would see it as a weakness and prey on it.

"We are not here to discuss him, sister." The sound of Stevie's voice sent ice down my spine. Her voice had changed. I know it sounds stupid, but it was deeper and sounded raspy. The girl standing in front of me wasn't my sister anymore. The darkness my father spoke of has clearly taken a hold over her faster than he thought. Were we too late to save her now?

"What would you like to discuss, then, coven queen?" Stevie snapped her gaze to Nico. Gone was the indifferent look she had been wearing; she was now glaring and shooting daggers at Nico with her eyes, her lips pulled back in a snarl.

"You do not get to fucking speak right now, you fucking bottom feeding cockroach." Ouch! That was fucking rude.

"That's no way to talk to your future brother-in-law, now is it?" if Stevie was shocked by Nico's admission, she didn't show it. Instead, she started laughing. I looked to Jax and Nico, confused, but they seemed no more in the know than I.

"My sister will never marry you, once she finds out what you did." I could see Nico out of the corner of my eye, and he didn't so much as flinch or react in any way to my sister's words.

His lack of reaction made me suspicious; an innocent person would have some form of reaction.

"You know nothing, witch; get to the point of your unwanted visit."

"I will speak to my sister privately."

"Yeah, that's not gonna happen."

"No one asked your opinion, Alpha; this is between me and my sister." I wanted to hear what my sister had to say, but I knew it would be difficult to get Nico to give me some space and time alone with her. I knew Nico was the more difficult of the two so I looked to Jax, pleading with my eyes that he give me some time with my sister. We stayed staring at each other for a long moment before Jax broke our little staring match.

"You have five minutes." I mouthed a silent *thank you* to Jax.

"Like fuck!" I knew Nico would make this difficult.

"Stone, give them five minutes." Now Jax and Nico were in a bloody stare off. Jax stalked over to Nico and gripped him by his arm; they were whisper arguing, and after that they took a step away from each other.

"Five minutes and not a second longer." I didn't verbalize my response to Nico, I only nodded, and they made their way back to the forest, with Nico turning back every couple steps like he wanted to change his mind and insist on staying with me.

I loved his protectiveness; it made me feel cared for, and I haven't felt like that before. Once they disappeared into the forest and I could no longer see their retreating forms, my sister finally spoke.

"Well, well, look at you, little sister." Stevie was looking me up and down with a disgusted look. "I see you are surviving well with the mutts and the fairies." I hated how Stevie was referring to the Pack and the Fae like they were beneath us; she was so wrong.

"One, you're older than me by a few minutes. Two, don't

speak about the Pack and the Fae like that. They're good people, Stevie, and they're innocent. Why do you hate them so much?"

"Because they are beneath me and need to learn their fucking place, like you do, sister." I saw Tyler flinch at the way she spoke about the pack; his reaction was disturbing. Why the hell would he care, when he was the one who turned his back on them to start with? Shaking myself out of my thoughts, I focused my full attention back on my sister.

"They are not beneath us, Stevie; they are just as important as the coven and the vampires."

"You are so fucking naïve, Ryan. No wonder mother dearest loved beating you." Her words fucking pierced me; Stevie knew what saying things like that did to me, and she was enjoying hurting me.

I couldn't let her see how much her words affected me. I took the advice she gave me the first night we arrived in Alaska: fake it till you make it.

"Get to the point of why you are here, Stevie." A sly smirk graced her face.

"Well, look who finally found their backbone." Wow, what a bitch. "You need to stand down and stop this fucking game you're playing. You will help us seal the fae realm. Those disgusting bastards killed our father. I guess you forgot that part, since you're marrying the king of fucking murderers!" My sister was so delusional; Nico didn't kill our father. I was starting to believe what my cousins said was right: maybe my sister was the one to end my father's life, or at the very least she had a hand in it.

"You don't get to tell me what to do, Stevie. I am not a child, and who I marry is none of your concern."

"Look at you, spreading your legs for anyone. First it was the leech, and now you're fucking the king of the people who killed our father. I'm sure Dad would be so proud of you, fucking his killer and all."

Fierce anger coursed through my veins. *How fucking dare she!* I have never wanted to hurt my sister physically except when I thought she killed Kai. And she thought she had the right to speak about Kai, after what she did to him? Stevie had no right to speak about our father, when she had no idea what the truth was. I started to feel really hot, and I could feel my magic rising within me.

I looked down and saw my hands glowing. This time I didn't freak out or try to calm down, I embraced the power running through my veins.

I walked toward my sister, leaving a foot of space between us. She didn't react to my display of power, and she seemed almost gleeful.

"You don't fucking ever speak about Kai, or *my* father again, you lying twisted bitch." She had the audacity to smile, and I lost it. I only meant to shove her back to release some of my pent-up anger, but instead I sent my sister sailing through the air. The wooden fence didn't stand a chance against the blast; the remains were mere splinters and my sister landed with a thud about a football field length away. Tyler ran to Stevie, but I didn't give a flying fuck if she was hurt.

She needed a taste of her own medicine. She liked to hurt and boss people around. I wouldn't let her do that to me anymore. No one was going to control me; I was finally free. I heard footsteps pounding the ground behind me, and I spun around to see Jax and Nico running toward me. I didn't want them to stop me; I wasn't done with my sister yet. I closed my eyes and called to the magic inside me, I envisioned a bubble so I could trap them inside of it.

I was shocked when I saw a dome of glimmering blue surround me, Tyler, and Stevie, but grateful that my power was starting to work with me instead of against me. I turned and started walking toward my sister and Tyler; the dome started shrinking as I drew closer to my sister. Once I was a few feet in front of her, I saw that her leg was at an odd angle and she wasn't moving. Tyler was checking her for a pulse, and it was then that I started to realize what I had done. Stevie wasn't the only monster now. I nearly killed my sister! The rage inside me was slowing and starting to ease, the more I looked at Stevie. What the fuck have I done?

CHAPTER 21

Ryan

"Oh my God, Stevie." I rushed over to her and knelt down beside her. Tyler started growling, but that didn't deter me. I rolled her over so she was lying on her back and put my ear to her mouth so I could hear if she was breathing. I didn't hear anything, so I started to do CPR. I kept pushing on her chest then blowing air into her mouth, but it wasn't working. I killed my sister! "You don't get to fucking die, Stevie, wake the fuck up now." She wasn't responding. Tears were running freely down my face, and I was sobbing so hard I could barely continue to perform CPR.

"Let him in." I looked to Tyler, confused.

"L-let w-who in?" I could barely talk past the lump in my throat. Tyler raised his hand and pointed behind me, and I turned to see who he was pointing at and gasped. Behind the dome I had erected stood Jax, Nico, Kai, and about twenty other men, who I was assuming were the shifters Jackson had stationed in the trees in case my sister ambushed us. Why the fuck was Kai here? I turned to Tyler.

"If you say anything to Randall about Kai..."

"You have my word Ryan, I will say nothing." I didn't trust

Tyler as far as I could throw him. The expression on my face must have conveyed what I was thinking.

"His blood can heal her. If she doesn't heal soon, she will die. She has internal bleeding." I looked down at my sister and saw no clear sign that she was bleeding internally. "I can feel her life draining."

"How?"

"You are not the only anomaly, Ryan. Your sister is my mate." Oh my God. That's why he left and betrayed us—he didn't have a choice.

"That's why you left, isn't it?"

"Yes"

"You have to help me stop her Tyler, she cannot do this. She will kill a whole world."

"What the fuck do you think I am doing? I don't want to fucking help her or Randall kill the fucking fae. Going against my pack and Jax is the hardest thing I have ever fucking done. My sister is back there, and I can't even fucking see her! If Stevie finds out I am trying to help you, she will not hesitate to kill me. Wolves don't mate outside of their race, but apparently I am the exception. Unfortunately, your sister doesn't feel the bond the way I do."

"She can't help it, she's changing."

"We don't have time for this. *She is dying.* Now will you help me or not?"

"Of course I will, she is my sister."

"Fucking break it down now," I snapped at Kai.

"I can't." Why the fuck was he here then if he couldn't help?

"You got near her last time when she blasted Randall's office; no one else could, but you did." It burned my tongue to say that shit out loud. I hated watching him be able to go to her while I was spying from the forest outside Randall's office.

"Her power has grown; she doesn't want us near her, so we can't penetrate the force field until she lets us. Maybe Dom can breach it?"

"Dom's not fucking here, Kai." I was about to lose my shit.

"Can you open a portal next to her?"

"You don't think I fucking tried that, Jackson? I can't breach the dome; nothing I have tried has worked!" I know I was being an ass, but I couldn't control my temper; Ryan was stuck in a force field of her own making with her evil fucking twin and the traitor. Tyler could hurt her, and there wasn't a fucking thing I could do about it.

"Alpha." All three of us looked to Lucas; he was Jax's go-to for war strategies.

"What is it, Lucas?" Jackson was using his alpha tone, which meant his wolf was in more control than he was.

"Maybe Lady Sophia can help?" *How the fuck does he know about my sister?*

"How do you know about my sister?" I saw Lucas tense and looked at the other pack members around him.

"Lady Sophia is very powerful and she helped us." *What has my sister been up to?* Before I could answer, Jackson spoke.

"I linked one of the pack members to bring Sophia here immediately." No sooner had Jax finished talking a portal open five feet from us. My sister walked through the portal with not a care in the world.

"So, I hear you need my help, brother."

"How can you help if I can't even breach the fucking force field, Soph? How did you open a portal?"

"I see you still doubt me, Nico. Dom opened the portal for me; he and the boys are back from the coven. Dom will join us shortly after they get Mya settled." I saw a look of hurt cross her face before she masked it. "Kai, you and I need to move to the northern side of the dome so she can see us. She will let us through."

"You're not fucking going anywhere, Sophia, and he sure as fuck isn't going anywhere with you."

"You either trust me or you don't, Nico" Sophia was looking me dead in the eyes, I couldn't get the words out of my mouth. I trusted my sister, right?

"Fuck, we don't have time for this, Sophia, let's go." I stood there stunned as Kai gripped my sister's arm and led her to the other side of the dome. Why the fuck couldn't I tell my sister that I trusted her?

"You just royally fucked up, your majesty." *Tell me something I don't already fucking know, Jackson.*

"Drop the force field."

"I don't know how Tyler."

"Are you fucking serious?" I flinched at his tone; I felt so stupid right in this moment. I made the damn fucking thing and now I couldn't even drop it.

"Figure it out fast, because they have reinforcements now." I turned to see a portal open and Sophia step through it. Oh no, this can't be good.

"Fuck, okay, give me a minute."

"We only have about a minute, so fucking hurry or your sister dies." Fuck, I closed my eyes and started to envision the dome going away, but every time I peeked an eye open, it was still there.

"You need to hurry, Ryan. If she dies, I will lose control over my wolf, and I will kill you." Oh God. I gulped so loudly I'm sure everyone outside of the dome heard it.

I closed my eyes and tried to concentrate really hard on the dome disappearing, but every time I opened my eyes, it was still there.

Tyler growling constantly didn't help the situation. I closed my eyes again and said a silent prayer to my dad, asking him to help me.

"Ryan!" I snapped my eyes open at the sound of Sophia's voice. She was outside the dome, behind Tyler.

"I can't drop the dome! Sophia, what do I do?" Sophia turned and whispered something in Kai's ear.

"Mi amor, I need you to focus on me and envision a small tear in the dome. Sophia is going to cast a spell to tear an opening in the dome, but you need to help her." I took a deep breath and nodded. Closing my eyes again, I envisioned a small tear in my mind's eye. I tuned out Tyler's growling and every other noise in the clearing, focusing only on causing a rip in the dome. "Keep going, mi amor, you're doing great." A moment later I felt a hand land on my shoulder and shrieked; I looked up to see Kai staring down at me. "You did great, mi amor, Now I need you to move so I can save your sister's life." I know this wasn't easy for Kai, after all my sister had done to him.

CHAPTER 24

We watched Sophia and Kai from our position on the other side of the dome. I had no idea what my sister had planned or how she was going to get through the dome, but I had to trust in her; she asked me to trust her, and that is what I am doing.

"What the hell is taking them so long?"

"Sophia said to trust her, Jax, so that is what I am doing. You should trust her too."

"She's changed, you know; she seems so different now." I couldn't agree with Jackson more, my sister isn't the same girl she was before she was taken many years ago. Every move she made now was well thought out and calculated. She was stronger and more fierce. There was something else, as well; I just couldn't quite put my finger on what it was exactly. "She did it! She and Kai are through."

I took off to the side of the dome where my sister and Kai had just gone through. Once we reached the side they had gone through, we felt around the dome for the opening.

"I can't find the entrance, Alpha."

"Me either, Alpha." I, Jax and his pack members were feeling everywhere for the opening but couldn't find one.

"She closed it." I turned and bared my teeth at one of the men; I didn't know who he was, but I didn't like his insinuation that Ryan had locked me out but allowed Kai entry. "I meant no disrespect your majesty."

"Don't worry about it, Kane, Nico is just on edge." Jackson was right; I was on edge and I needed to calm down. I looked back to Ryan and saw Kai place a hand on her shoulder. I could see their mouths moving but I couldn't hear shit. Ryan moved from her spot beside her sister and let Kai take her place. What the fuck are they doing? I didn't realize I had voiced my thought until Jackson answered me.

"Kai is saving her sister." I turned to Jackson and then back to the others in the dome. He was right. Kai is saving Ryan's sister—but why?

"Why the hell would he save the bitch that tried to kill him?" Jackson sighed and then placed a hand on my shoulder.

"For someone so old and apparently wise, you really are thick, aren't you?" I turned to glare at him, only for him to chuckle. "He may have manipulated her feelings for him, but his feelings for her are real."

"What the fuck does that even mean, Jackson?"

"It means that he loves her enough to save the life of the woman that tortured him and tried to kill him." Well, fuck, Kai is a bigger man than I. I don't think I could do what he is doing right now. Thinking back to the state he was in when Tyler brought him back sent a shiver down my spine. I don't know anyone else who could have withstood that type of torture and not snitch like a rat. I really needed to get over my jealousy with Kai and Ryan. What he did for her I can never repay; he was there for her when I wasn't. He tried to protect her as best as he could, and that made him the better man. He may be the better man, but I was the right man, and I would never give her up, no matter what. When he finds out what she did to bring him back, I wonder if he will still feel the same way about her then?

CHAPTER 25

Ryan

It feels like hours have passed since Kai bit his wrist and fed his blood to Stevie, but in reality it was mere minutes.

"We need to reset her leg so it doesn't heal wrong." I didn't even think about her leg, but Tyler was right—it was at such an odd angle that there was no way it would heal right.

"How do we do that?"

"It's okay. I can cast a small spell to set it straight."

"Thank you, Sophia." I then turned to Kai, only to find him staring straight back at me. "Thank you for doing this; I know this can't be easy for you, and I appreciate you doing it. I owe you for saving my sister, Kai."

"I owe you as well." Both Kai and I turned to face Tyler, shocked at his admission. "You didn't have to save her after everything she did."

"I didn't do it for her or for you."

"I know, Melakai, but I still owe you a debt." Kai didn't respond verbally to Tyler, but gave him a curt nod.

"Okay, I'm going to move her leg now and then cast the spell before Kai's blood starts to heal it." We all nodded and followed Sophia's direction on how to move my sister's leg. I winced when I heard a crack as we straightened it. "Okay, that's fine, now step back." We did as instructed, and Sophia started chanting a spell under her breath. Tyler moved to sit by Stevie's head so he could place her head in his lap. Minutes passed before Stevie even started to stir, and I released the breath I didn't know I was holding. *What happens now? I think I just made everything worse by hurting my sister; I doubt we're going to have a peace talk now.*

"What happens now?" I didn't ask anyone in particular. I was just voicing my inner thoughts.

"Once she is conscious, I will take her home."

"Tyler, you need to help me convince her; what she is doing is wrong and you know it."

"She won't change her mind, Ryan."

"You underestimate your importance to her, wolf." Tyler snapped his eyes to Sophia. He was shocked she even knew about him and my sister.

"How did you know about Stevie and me?"

"I see others love lives—long story. Anyway you need to stay by her side." Okay, so now Sophia was being cryptic as shit. All conversation stopped when I heard shouting from outside the dome. I turned to where the guys were standing and saw Dom and my cousins had joined our audience. I gave them a small wave. What can I say? I'm an awkward fucker.

"So, how do we get out of this thing?" I was looking between my three companions, seeing which one of them would have an idea. By the looks on their faces, they had no fucking clue. Great. "Can we try doing that tear thing again?"

"My magic is low at the moment. I used a lot to help you open the tear and then heal your sister's leg." Oh right, Kai couldn't do magic, so he was out of the question. Tyler was a shifter, so he was out too. I guess we needed my cousins or Dom. Wait—why wasn't Nico helping us?

"Why didn't Nico break through the dome? I mean, I am glad you both did, but I thought he would have busted in here by now."

"Nico can't penetrate your dome." I started blushing and giggling at Sophia's words. Yeah I know, I needed to get my head out of the gutter. I heard Tyler muttering something about being real mature, but I ignored him. Clearing my throat, I looked to Sophia and asked,

"What do we do now?"

"I think we may need to ask your cousins and Dom for help." Sophia seemed reluctant to have to involve Dom, but everyone knew there was a story with them. I wanted to figure it out. They would make the cutest couple. I walked past Sophia with Kai hot on my heels, heading toward Dom and my cousins. Before we reached them, I turned to Kai.

"Thank you for saving my sister, Kai. I know that must have been hard for you." Kai didn't stop or look at me; he just continued walking toward the group outside of the dome.

"I didn't do it for her."

I felt like a piece of shit asking Kai to save Stevie, but I didn't have another choice. My sister was dying, and I knew Kai could save her. I was a fucking terrible person. As we reached the edge of the dome, my steps faltered, seeing Nico looking so angry. His body was tense and his face was contorted in harsh lines. His violet eyes were so dark they were almost blue, and his lips were pulled back in a snarl. Right. So clearly Nico was pissed he was outside the dome and not inside of it. Whoops.

"So on a scale of one to ten, how mad are you right now?" I tried for humor, hoping that would ease some of the anger coursing through Nico.

"You think this is funny, little one?" Okay, I guess my humor didn't work. Nico was *pissed*.

"It's not her fault." Nico turned to Kai, glaring. If his eyes could shoot laser beams, I'm sure he would have done it. Wait, *can* he shoot laser beams?

"You—" Nico stopped talking and then yelled to the heavens, no one spoke as we watched him pace a small line back and forth for a moment. I have never seen Nico this worked up before, it was quite scary. "You are trapped in a fucking force field of your own making with your bitch of a sister, who wants to kill you and nearly killed my best friend, and you think this is a fucking joke?" I reassessed my need to leave my protective bubble. Nico was *hot*.

"Nico, calm down, this isn't helping anyone." At least Dom was thinking straight. "Melakai, how did you and Sophia get in?"

"You men are so dumb." I turned to look over my shoulder to see Sophia had joined us. Fuck, she was quiet. I didn't even hear her approach.

"What the fuck is that supposed to mean, Sophia?"

"It means, brother, none of you have done the simplest thing."

"What *is* the simple thing then, little dove?" Soph turned her gaze to Dom and smiled.

"I simply *asked* her to let us in." Well, technically Kai asked. All the males outside of the dome turned to look at each other like Sophia had said the most outrageous thing in the world. Chase and Alex just laughed; my cousins knew I hated it when I was told to do something instead of being asked. I think Sophia's answer had merit; my power seemed to be so in tune with me at the moment. She did ask me to let her in, and my power allowed it. Nico, on the other hand demands everything, and I hate that, so of course my power wouldn't allow him entry. I needed to get this power thing sorted ASAP. So much shit was riding on me, and it was starting to weigh me down. My power was the key to stopping Randall, because he had ingested the blood of the previous alpha and coven king, my dad. My power was the only thing to save my sister from the darkness inside of her. My blood was the key to grant vampires the ability to walk in the daylight without ever having to feed off another fae. One drop of my blood and they were set for life. My whole life was a cluster fuck at the moment, and I couldn't see an end in sight. Nico's voice pulled me from my inner turmoil.

"Little one, can you let me in now, please?" I could tell it hurt his ego to have to ask such a thing and I must admit that made me feel quite triumphant.

"Yeah, that's easier said than done." Nico was glaring at me now. "Stop looking at me like that; it's not like I have a fucking manual on how to navigate these powers."

"You let my sister and *him* in." Called it. He's jealous.

"Stop getting pissy, Nico. Give me a second to think." I turned to Kai and Sophia. "When you asked to come in, I thought of a tear in the dome and then suddenly you both were inside. Is that what I do again?"

"I cast a spell to help the tear open. My magic is low so you would have to—"

"We'll do it." I turned back to face the others and saw it was Chase who spoke. "We are capable of doing it, Ry. Dom can't at the moment." Wait, why couldn't Dom do it? What was wrong with him?

"Dom, why can't you do it?" Dom wouldn't meet my eyes, and I had a sinking feeling something had happened when he went to the Knox coven to retrieve Mya.

"We're running out of time! Stevie is starting to wake, and if you don't get this fucking thing down she will go ape shit, Ryan." Oh fuck, I could hear the panic in Tyler's voice, I needed to hurry.

"Okay, Chase, what do you need me to do?"

"I need you to think of the dome disappearing, Ry. Alex and

I can only help you shrink it, but we can't make it go away. It's too strong." I followed Chase's instructions and closed my eyes, envisioning the dome disappearing. It was hard to concentrate when I could hear Jax, Dom, and Nico talking among them.

"If you three can't shut your cake holes for five fucking minutes, you need to leave! You are distracting her." I was starting to like Sophia more and more; she was my kind of girl. I closed my eyes and started to think of the dome disappearing. Sweat broke out across my brow. I could feel something was happening inside me, my body was starting to warm. I couldn't open my eyes to see if it was working, afraid if I did it would stop.

"That's it, mi amor, keep going, you're doing great." Kai's words of encouragement helped boost my confidence. I focused harder on drawing the magic back inside me.

 Nico

She was doing it! The dome was getting smaller and smaller. I could see by the strain on her face it was taking a toll on her. She was doing fucking amazing. I just wished I was by her side instead of Kai. I should be the one there holding her hand and whispering words of encouragement instead of him. I know she doesn't feel the same way about him anymore, but my jealousy knows no bounds. She was my ever after, and he was a threat to that. What if I told her the truth and she chose him? I wouldn't survive that. She was mine, and I would make her see that. I had to show her that I was the better man and the right choice. She was my *hugacko* and nothing would change that.

"Keep going, Ryan, you're doing it." Jackson's voice snapped me from my thoughts. The dome had shrunk; it was only covering Ryan now, and Sophia and Kai moved back a step. I don't think they wanted to be trapped in the dome again.

Moving my gaze from Ryan to her sister and Tyler, they were surrounded by at least ten of Jackson's men in wolf form.

Shifters were at their strongest when they were in their beast form.

"Keep going, love, nearly there," Dom encouraged her. I watched as the last of her force field shrunk inside of her. She opened her eyes, looking around, and then started to sway. I shot forward and caught her just as she collapsed in my arms.

"I got you, baby." I kept one arm wrapped around the base of her neck while scooping her legs up with the other, cradling her against my chest. She looked so worn out.

"What should we do with her sister and Tyler?" Dom posed a great question, what do we do with them?

"Jax, do you still have the holding cells I made for your father?" Many years ago, I made Jackson's father some holding cells; they were strong enough to hold a shifter, and the iron bars I used muted fae magic. I also cast a powerful spell to mute any witch's or warlock's magic, as well.

"Yeah, but do you think it's a good idea to hold them, though?"

"Do you really think letting the bitch that tried to kill Kai and oh, hang on, wants to kill my whole fucking world, go free is a good idea, Jackson?" Seriously, Jackson was working my last fucking nerve. Jax started growling and baring his teeth. As much as I would love to throw down with Jackson and release some pent-up anger, now wasn't the time with Ryan passed out in my arms. "If you want to hit the gym later and spar, I will be happy to oblige, Jax. Right now isn't the fucking time, though."

"Nico's right, Jax." At least Dom was seeing some fucking sense. "We need to question her sister and find out what the fuck she and Randall are planning."

After leaving the others to deal with Stevie and Tyler, I made my way back to the compound. I laid Ryan down in her bed and sat next to her, gently stroking her hair.

"When you find out what I have been hiding, please don't hate me, little one. I only did it so I could protect my people. I thought giving Randall your mother would grant my sister's freedom and put an end to this war, but I was wrong. I didn't know you back then; I didn't know then what I know now." I heard someone gasp behind me and quickly stood so I could face the intruder—or intruders, in this case. I stood there staring at both Ryan's cousins.

"What the fuck have you done, Tink?" Shit. They heard. Fuck.

"I can explain..."

"You better fucking start explaining now!" Alex was yet to say a word. Chase, on the other hand, had no problem hurling insults at me. "You are a fucking lying piece of shit. Our father told us that fae were honorable people and couldn't lie; clearly he was wrong."

"Technically we can't lie." I was trying to stall so I could come up with a good excuse, anything was better than the truth at this point.

"All you have done is lie to her." Chase had a valid point, I haven't exactly been very honest.

"Nico, I have heard nothing but good things about you from

our father and our uncle. You are starting to make me regret ever believing a word they said." I felt guilt at Alex's admission; this wasn't who I am as a person.

"I never meant to hide these things from her, but the more time that passed, the harder it got to tell her the whole story." I felt exposed admitting my feelings to the warlocks.

"She is more understanding than you give her credit for. She has been through hell at the hands of her mother. It is going to destroy her when she finds out you lied to her, again. What did you do with Nina?" Fuck, I had to tell them now.

"Nina left on her own accord, I swear. I just intercepted her. I thought that taking her and trading her to Randall would grant my sister's freedom."

"Why would Randall want Nina?"

"Because, Chase, he didn't know about Ryan then. I thought if I could give him the child of the queen, that would be the end of it."

"Why do you look like you just ate a lemon, Tink?" I really hated that fucking nickname from Chase. I glared at the bastard. "Stop stalling and spill now!"

"Nina sang like a canary and told Randall she had twins. Randall knew about the prophecy. He had planned to take Ryan from you at that party but couldn't. He saw how strong she was. He also knew when Kai was able to get her when she blew his office apart that Kai had feelings for her. He couldn't rely on Kai to control her emotions. Stevie made it easy for him when she had planned to lock you three up."

"I get what you're saying, but Ryan won't be that mad. It's not like she loves her Mom." Alex really was the smart one; he knew I was holding back. Ryan is going to hate me.

"When Randall realized Ryan was real, he cut the deal off and wouldn't let Sophia go. He changed the terms of the deal and said I had to give him Ryan in exchange for my sister." Both Chase and Alex looked like they wanted to kill me, but I wasn't finished yet. "I told Randall I couldn't do it, and I was gonna figure out a different way to get my sister back. Randall started sending parts of Ryan's mother to me for my betrayal. I swear, I have been trying to get her mother back, I know she hates her, but at the end of the day, that is still her Mom."

"You bastard. You were going to trade Ryan, weren't you?" I can't directly lie when someone asks me a question. I took a deep breath. It was time I admit how much of a piece of shit I am.

"The thought did cross my mind. I had searched for my sister for years, and no matter what I did, Randall was always a step ahead somehow. You have to understand I didn't know Ryan well when I considered Randall's new trade."

"You lying piece of shit!" I spun around to see Ryan sitting up in her bed shooting a death glare my way. "You planned to trade me for Sophia?" I started shaking my head, ready to try explain myself, but she wasn't having that. "That I do understand, but taking my mother and lying about it? I have looked for her for months, and this whole fucking time you knew where she was! I don't like my mother, but she is still my mother, and you handed her over to the fucking devil himself."

"I...I...sorry." Fuck, I couldn't even put a sentence together. She was never supposed to find out like this.

"Sorry? I can't with you Nico. You have lied to me for the last fucking time. You knew where my mother was and never told me. Wait. My mother was at Randall's mansion when I was, wasn't she?" I didn't bother to speak, I just nodded. "Get the fuck out and stay the fuck out of my sight, Nico." I lowered my head and stood rooted to the floor for a minute, after a long inhale of air I turned and started to leave the room. Just as I opened the door ready to step out, she spoke. "You were right, you know." I turned and looked back over my shoulder.

"I was right about what?"

"Kai was definitely the better choice and better man." Well, fuck me, hearing that felt like a dagger to the heart.

CHAPTER 27

Ryan

I asked my cousins to leave as soon as Nico did. Once again I needed time alone to process the information that had been kept from me. I could understand Nico wanting to trade my life for his sister, that wasn't the problem. I was angry that he lied about it. He knew where my mother was the whole time. He never once mentioned while I was at Randall's mansion that my mother was there, that she was being tortured. I am so beyond hurt and angry. I just started to trust him and then he goes and pulls this shit. How am I supposed to forgive him? Once a liar always a liar.

I was sitting in the single chair by the window, looking out at the beautiful Alaskan scenery. It was so beautiful here. I loved the cool, crisp air in the morning. I could live here. I started thinking that I might actually do it, after all this shit is over with that dick Randall.

I might just move here. I knew Nico wanted me to live with him in the fae realm, but that wasn't going to happen. We would get married as planned, unlock my powers, finish this fight with Randall, and then go our separate ways.

Why did the thought of leaving Nico and never seeing him again cause an ache in my chest?

I knew I had feelings for him, that much was obvious, but you couldn't build a relationship on just feelings. You needed communication and trust. I didn't trust Nico, and we sure as shit didn't really communicate. I still found it gross that Nico was supposed to marry my grandmother. I mean, come on, that is fucked up, right? I knew Nico and the other three guys were way older, but how much older than me are they?

Questions like these are banking up. I know they're trivial, but there are things I felt like I should know. I need to find someone who could answer these questions—maybe Sophia?

I was pulled from my thoughts by a knock at the door; I didn't bother to move, just told whoever it was to come in.

Holy shit, did I somehow mind link her or something? Sophia and Aurora walked in, closing the door behind them.

"So is this how you plan to spend your last day as a single woman?" I hadn't actually thought about that.

"Um...no?" I didn't mean to sound so unsure, but what were my options, really? It's not like I actually had any friends that would want to throw me a party. I saw a look of pity on Aurora's face, but Sophia's held a look of determination. Oh no, that could only mean trouble. Sophia made her way over to me and grabbed my wrist, pulling me to my feet in one fluid motion. "What are you doing, Sophia?"

"Well, you're not going to sit around here and wallow in self-pity. My brother's a dick. Get over it, you're still marrying him." Wow, she really didn't mince words, did she? At least she agreed that her brother was a dick. I decided right here and now that I like Sophia, a lot.

"We have a suggestion." I looked past Sophia to see Aurora; she seemed hesitant.

"Okay, why do you look like you ate a lemon, Aurora?"

Sophia sighed, I turned to look at her, waiting for her to answer instead of Aurora.

"Fine! We're taking you to see your sister." Wait, what?

"Where the hell is my sister?"

"In the cells. Now, if you want to see her, you need to hurry up." I nodded to Sophia and quickly followed both the girls out of my room and down a zigzagging maze of hallways. We emerge from the building to a side of the compound I had never seen. It was barren and dark from the shade of the huge trees, and I felt uncomfortable being on this side. There was no warmth to be found from the sun, only darkness. "Hurry up and stay behind me." I nodded. We began walking toward an old shack; it looked really old. If a strong gust of wind came, it would probably blow it over. When we reached the front of the shack, Sophia knocked on an old, wooden door.

"Who is it?" Hey, I know that voice.

"Open the fucking door, Dom, it's cold as shit out here."

"How cold does shit get, little dove?" I could hear the humor in Dom's voice. Sophia didn't answer Dom, she growled instead. Holy shit, she could give a shifter a run for their money with that growl. You could hear laughter coming from the other side of the door before it was opened. Sophia pushed past Dom and made her way inside, and, not wanting to freeze my ass off, I quickly followed. Dom shut the door as soon as Aurora entered. The room is tiny; with just four of us inside, it was a tight fit. Looking between my three companions, I asked.

"Where's my sister?"

Dom just smiled and said, "Hold on love, she's below us."

Huh?

Dom placed his hand on the side of the wall and we started to descend. Oh my God, the room was a secret elevator. "If we had prisoners sitting above ground, anyone could try setting them free. Doing it this way, the elevator only works with certain magic signatures and palm prints." That was freaking smart, no one could break in and try stealing the prisoners.

"So, who can get to people below us?"

"Jax, Nico, Kai, and two of Jax's trusted guards, and well, of course, me." I didn't respond as the elevator came to a halt. Dom opened the wooden door we entered through above ground and exited. We followed Dom out, and I was shocked.

There was proper lighting down here and the walls weren't made of dirt or rock but rather concrete.

Walking further along, I saw quite a few cells, the bars on them seemed thicker than normal prisons—well, ones that I had seen on TV, and they were a darker color as well. We walked another minute and turned a small corner, and I stopped dead in my tracks. The cell at the end of the hall held my sister. She was sitting on a makeshift bed made out of a concrete slab. Her brown hair was a tousled mess, and her posture showed me how defeated she felt. I rushed past Dominic and stopped right in front of my sister's cell. She didn't lift her head or even acknowledge our presence.

"What's wrong with her? What happened to my sister?" The person that answered wasn't one that I expected; I turned my head to look at the cell next to my sister and saw Tyler.

"She draws her power from nature. Being so far underground and surrounded by concrete blocks that off."

"Open the door, I want to go in." I needed to make sure she was okay. I know Stevie has done some fucked-up shit, but she was still my sister.

"I can't do that, love." I turned to glare at Dom. How fucking dare he bring me down here and then deny me a chance to sit with my sister and try fix things?

"Open the fucking door Dom, I want to—" I stopped speaking immediately and spun around to face my sister when I heard her voice. She was still sitting in the same place, with her head hanging low.

"You can't come in here, Ryan."

"Why not, Stevie? I want to help you."

"You can't help me!" She snapped her head up and locked her gaze on mine. That's when I saw it—the darkness I saw in her eyes earlier had receded. Her being down here was a good thing, I think. She was cut off from all magic, which meant the darkness inside couldn't get to her down here.

"Stevie, I need to explain things to you, Dad told me..."

"You think I don't know about the darkness inside me? I have known all along, Ryan. Dad tried to hide it from me. Mya told me the truth. Oh and don't think that I don't know you took her from the coven." I gasped. How the hell did she know that? If Stevie knew all along why didn't she try to get help?

After leaving Ryan's room, I wandered around the compound for a while, trying to sort through my thoughts. I had no idea where I was going, I just couldn't stay in one place at the moment. I don't know how I wound up outside Jackson's office door. I was kind of glad that I did, I could use someone to talk to. I knocked, waiting for him to invite me in. When he did, I opened the door and entered. Jackson wasn't alone; Melakai was sitting on one of the couches, gazing out the window.

"I'll come back later." I turned to leave, only to be stopped by Kai's words.

"I'm sorry." I thought I might have misheard him, I turned to face him. "I shouldn't have tricked Ryan. I thought if I did, I could save her from all of this." With a long exhale, I made my way over to the other couch and took a seat. Jackson moved out from behind his desk and sat in one of the single chairs.

"I get why you did it, I just don't like that you did it."

"I didn't know what she was to you back then." I turned to look at Jackson, he at least had the decency to look sheepish. "Don't blame Jackson, he told me the truth so I would back off and leave you and her be." I was shocked, to say the least.

"Thank you?"

"Don't sound so shocked Nico, if you had of told me from the start she was your hugacko, I never would have continued what I was...doing."

"Don't lie to me, Kai—you would never have stopped." He finally pulled his gaze from the window to look at me. Kai had changed since he came back; his eyes told you how haunted he was on the inside.

"I love her, Nico, but you are my brother. I would never try to destroy your bond with her. She is yours, not mine." I heard the pain in his voice. He didn't want to admit that Ryan was mine. I respected Kai so much right now, I know this can't be easy for him.

"Okay, both of you, do know she is not an object? She can't be owned." Both Kai and I snapped our gaze to Jax. "Don't look at me like that, either of you. This is why she is always pissed at the pair of you." I looked to Kai, who looked just as confused as me.

"What do you mean, Jax?"

"My God, Nico, you are thick. She hates that you both talk about her like she can be owned. She has lived through a horror story, her mother wanted to own her and control her. Her sister tried to control her. She finally got away from her mother when you kidnapped—"

"I didn't kidnap her, I just borrowed her." Both Kai and Jax glared at me. Yeah, okay, that was a piss weak attempt at sticking up for myself. Jax, Dom, and Kai knew what I had done with Ryan's mother, I told Dom and Jax after I realized Kai knew.

"Anyway, she was finally free, then all this shit happened and you two dicks are trying to do the same thing her mother did to her."

"Fuck." Yeah, what Kai said. I was doing the thing she hated most. Jackson had a satisfied look on his face as he saw realization dawn on our faces. Fucking smug prick, I'll give him a taste of his own medicine.

"So Jax, how are things with Aurora?" Jackson's expression changed immediately.

"Fuck you, Nico, you don't get to ask me about her." Yeah, that was a dick move on my part.

"Jax, I really am sorry. I only wanted to help Aurora."

"Help her, why?" And he said I was thick.

"Because she said you would fucking die, dumb ass." He recoiled at my outburst, but a look of understanding crossed his face. He knew I cast the spell to try and save him, not hurt him.

"I understand, Nico, but don't interfere with my love life again. You have enough interference in your own to worry about." Bastard was bloody right, but that didn't mean I liked to hear it. We sat there talking about good memories and mending bridges between us that were damaged from our time apart.

Shit might suck right now because Randall discovered Ryan, but I will always be grateful, because her coming here brought me and my brothers back together again.

It felt so good to sit here and have a few whiskeys with my brothers and laugh about dumb shit. Just as I started to pour our third glass, I stilled at Kai's confession.

"I wish you well tomorrow, brother, but I cannot be there." I finished pouring our drinks and carried them over to the guys and sat back down.

"Why can't you be there, Kai?"

"I will not face Randall until I am at full strength. I will not be able to tame the urge to kill him if he is in my sight." I could feel the anger radiating off Kai—now that he was free from his blood oath to the vampire king, he wanted vengeance.

"I understand, brother."

"No you don't, Nico, you have no idea how hard it was to stand by and not be able to do a thing while he hurt Ryan's grandmother and then to watch and not be able to help Sophia. That killed me every day." I tensed as soon as he mentioned my sister. Soph wouldn't disclose any information about what happened to her. She was with Randall for seventeen years and suffered untold torture. "She is not the same woman who was captured, Nico. Sophia is stronger than you could ever imagine." I knew he was right; So-So was definitely stronger.

"You're right, I won't sit here and say that I am heartbroken over the queen's death. She knew the risk of leaving the fae realm with Randall and what it would mean for her people if she didn't go through with the marriage to me. I know, deep down inside of me, she was the one who told Randall how to enter my realm.

Her doing that caused my sister to be taken. I will kill that son of a bitch for what he did to Sophia. I'm getting married tomorrow, Kai, and I really wish you would change your mind and be there with me; I want my brothers by my side."

I could see Kai was torn; he wanted to be there for me, but wasn't sure if he could control his urge to kill Randall. I did something that I don't normally do to sway his decision.

"Please."

"How could I say no when you asked so nicely?" Fucking prick.

"Okay, guys, I don't mean to break up this heart to heart, but one of my guys has just told me he saw Ryan, Sophia and Aurora enter the cells."

"It won't matter, Jax, they can't get down there."

"Actually, Nico, they already have."

"How the fuck did they get down there?"

"Dom" That one name from Jax's lips sent my blood boiling. Fucking Dominic. I was going to beat his fucking ass. He was going too far these days and needed to be taught a fucking lesson.

CHAPTER 29

"Stevie, if you knew this whole time, why didn't you say anything? We could have tried to help you!"

"I don't want your fucking help, Ryan! I am the queen of the Knox coven."

Is she fucking serious right now? That's all she cared about — being queen.

"Everyone knows you're the fucking queen, Stevie! I don't care about that, I care about you! I'm trying to save you from yourself, not take some fucking crown from you!" Stevie jumped to her feet, glaring at me, and made her way over to the cell door, where I stood.

"You will never get my crown, Ryan!" Okay, so maybe I was wrong. Her being down here didn't completely take away her psycho side. I leaned in closer, so we were nearly nose to nose through the bars.

"If me taking the fucking crown from you is what is going to save you, then I will. I will find a way to help you, Stevie. Dad told me there's a way. This darkness inside of you is going to kill you. I will not let you hurt yourself or anyone else again! What you did to Melakai fucking disgusted me!"

A cruel smile graced her face, a face that I knew all too well. I saw that face every time I looked in the mirror. Her eyes started to darken; they weren't green anymore but rather a muddy brown. She straightened up and looked down her nose at me; The way she was looking at me sent shivers down my spine.

"I enjoyed breaking him. I loved hearing his screams." I recoiled at her words, and Dom surged forward and put his arm through the cell bars and gripped my sister around her throat, lifting her off the concrete floor. Tyler was shouting for him to put her down and hurling death threats at Dom.

"Dom please put her down." I was begging him to listen.

"You vile, fucking bitch. I will fucking kill you for what you did to my brother! I would love nothing more than to submit you to the pain you caused him. You're a fucking cunt!"

"Dominic! Put her down now!" Dom dropped Stevie immediately, and we all spun around at the sound of Nico's voice. Nico looked so angry. "What the fuck are you doing down here?"

"Calm down, brother."

"Don't fucking tell me to calm down, Sophia. That bitch has tried to kill Ryan, and you bring her down here, for what?"

"We brought her down here so she could deal with her demons, Nico."

"Shut the fuck up, Dominic! You and I are fucking going to have it out for this stunt!" Dom just smiled at Nico, almost like he had been waiting a long time for this showdown to happen.

"Fuck....you....all." I spun around at the sound of my sister's voice; she was still gasping for air and rubbing her throat. "Randall....and....I...will...kill..you all."

"Randall is a liar, Stevie!" She was so blinded by rage and this darkness inside her that she couldn't see the truth.

"He hasn't lied about anything, Ryan."

"He has Mom, Stevie." Stevie smiled a cruel smile. Holy shit, she knew all along. I took a step back, shaking my head. She knew this whole fucking time and said nothing? She knew I was still searching for our mother.

"You think I didn't know, sister? Of course I knew. When Randall offered me the chance to side with him and seal the fae realm, I took it. Then he told me he had that cunt that gave birth to us, and I told him I would join his crusade if he let me torture the bitch! How'd you like those body parts, Your Majesty?" Stevie started laughing like a maniac. Fuck, I think I was going to be sick. I turned to the side and gripped the bars on a vacant cell and started to dry heave. I felt a hand rub up and down my back. I didn't turn to see who it belonged to. "Oh my, look who it is, Melakai fucking Cane, prince to the vampire race."

"You don't get to speak to him, you bitch!"

"Oh, Sophia Stone, princess of the fae. You seem quite fond of the vampire, are you fucking him too? You seem to have recovered nicely since we last saw each other." Dom started growling, and I turned my head to see it was him rubbing my back. I straightened and cleared my throat. I knew what I had to do now; I could only save one of them, and the one I wanted to save the least was probably the only one I could save. That realization nearly broke me, but I wouldn't give up hope that I could save them both. I looked toward Tyler's cell, seeing Aurora cling to her brother's arm. Tyler's gaze met mine, and he was begging me to help him save my sister, and I nodded.

"We need to leave now."

"Come on Ryan, don't leave now, we were just getting to the fun part. Don't you want to know how mommy is doing? You know she asks for you, sister. Come visit her while she's still breathing, at least then you can say you saw one parent before they died." I turned and glared at my sister. I was fighting so hard to hold my tears back. I would not let my sister see me break.

"I will find a way to save you from yourself, Stevie, and when I do, you will be on your own." My sister's manic laughter followed us all the way to the exit.

Once we left the cells and made it back to Jackson's office, there was a small slender woman with white blonde hair sitting in the single chair by the couches.

"Who the hell are you?"

"That would be Mya, Squirt." I turned to see both Alex and Chase sitting on the other couch. I was shocked that this lady was Mya. "She's not what you expected, is she Squirt?" I had no words, I just shook my head. Mya wasn't old like I thought her to be.

"The joys of immortality, Miss Knox." She has a Southern accent, and she was so not what I had pictured. She had long, white blonde hair, a color girls these days were paying huge money to achieve, but it was her natural color. She had muddy brown eyes that radiated kindness. "Do not let my appearance fool you, Miss Knox. I am as old as these four men." I raised my brows in surprise; she appeared so youthful and put together.

"Ryan, meet Mya." I looked to Chase and then back to Mya,

still in shock. Mya smiled and made her way over to me. She extended her hand and I stood there like a stunned deer, staring at her hand. "Ry, you're supposed to shake the poor woman's hand."

"Right." I placed my hand inside hers and shook it. "It's a pleasure to meet you, Mya."

"The pleasure is all mine, Miss Knox." She released my hand and stepped back. "It is a pleasure to meet you all." Everyone said hello and introduced themselves, but Mya seemed to know everyone. We all took a seat on the couches and stared at each other. I don't think anyone knew what to say. Mya cleared her throat then looked to me. "Would you like to tell me why I am here, Miss Knox?"

"Um...I got a letter from my dad that said you could help me."

"Ask me what you wish to know, Miss Knox." She was so formal.

"Please just call me Ryan."

"Okay, Ryan, what would you like to know?"

"I want to know about my mother and about my sister and I...I want to know how to save my sister." Mya nodded her head and looked around the room.

"Would you like to have this conversation in private?"

"No," snapped Nico. I turned to glare at him and he backed off.

"I mean, I think you would like us to stay for support, right?" Nico was looking at Jackson, who was nodding his head like he was encouraging a toddler. These guys are fucking ridiculous.

"Squirt, if you want to have this conversation alone, we will all leave, even the fucking fairy." Nico turned to glare at Chase.

"It's fine, Mya, please continue."

"Okay, so I'll start from the beginning. It's a long story, are you sure you want to hear all of this the night before your wedding?" it wasn't even a hard question for me, I needed answers. I knew it was getting late and everyone would be tired but I didn't care, they could leave but I was staying.

"I need answers Mya, please. If any of you want to leave and get dinner or go to bed, you can." There was a chorus of *no* and *no thank you*. Jackson said he would get some pack members to deliver dinner to his office, which I appreciated, as I was starving. I needed food as soon as possible or I would start to get hangry, and no one needed me acting like a bitch during all this.

We decided to wait till dinner arrived before we started our chat, filling the time with chit chat about the coven and general catching up. Dinner arrived ten minutes later and we all polished off our plates within a few minutes.

"Okay now that we are all full and Ryan isn't gonna hulk out on us, we can start" I raised my middle finger to Chase but smiled sweetly at Mya and said, "Shall we begin?"

I had never met Mya before; I was just as shocked as Ryan to see her youthful appearance. Mya's eyes held so much wisdom and knowledge.

"Right, your father came to me fifteen years ago, so I could help him find a way to save your mother, and help him find a way to save you and your sister." This was news to me. "He figured out that your mother was cursed not long after she had given birth."

"The child was never cursed!" Mya didn't look pissed off or angry at Kai's outburst, she almost seemed like she expected it.

"Ryan's grandmother didn't intentionally curse her own daughter Melakai, it was an accident."

"The queen put a spell on the child to protect it from harm."

"Yes, Melakai, she did. Somehow the spell backfired when the queen's daughter had children of her own, I'm not sure how or why it happened."

"So you're saying my mother changed, because she had children?"

"Yes Ryan that is exactly what I'm saying."

"How did my dad figure this out?"

"He didn't at first; your mother was fine and happy. Then over time she started to get worse and your father grew concerned. He came to the coven to seek answers. I offered to help my king. We went through so many books and legends and came to the conclusion that your mother was the long-lost child of the queen. It was a story most of us knew but didn't believe it held any merit, until one day it did."

"How did you figure out that the spell my grandmother cast backfired?" Ryan was asking great questions, questions I think we all had.

"We don't know for sure how it backfired, but our guess is that the cell that she was held in was spelled by a powerful rogue witch, and when she cast her spell to protect her child, the witch's spell must have held some sort of failsafe. I don't really know how to explain it; sometimes when you cast a powerful spell there is a price to pay. If the spell the witch cast was powerful enough, and your grandmother cast her own, maybe the two different types of magic didn't agree and caused a ripple of some kind."

"Kai did tell me that my grandmother's cell was spelled." I looked over to Melakai to see him nodding. So that's why Kai could never break her out. Everyone called her queen, but the truth was she was only queen of the vampires, not the fae, as we never married.

"How do we save Stevie from herself?" Chase asked.

"That question, Mr. Knox, is a hard one to answer. I have searched high and low for years trying to find a sure way to save Miss Knox from the darkness inside her."

"So you're saying that there isn't a way?"

"I am saying, Mr. Knox, that there is a way to save her." I saw Ryan's eyes start to glisten; she had hope now that her sister could be saved. "If Stevie has accepted the darkness and embraced it, then no, she cannot be saved. If Stevie is still inside, fighting it, then yes, I believe she can be saved." Ryan's shoulders dropped and her face deflated, the tiny hope she had just got squashed.

"My dad told me that if I can control my powers, I can blast the darkness out of her."

"That is what we originally thought, Ryan. I kept looking into it after your father left, There is no research or books on this. We have never had something like this come about, before now." Ryan looked crestfallen; she thought Mya would give her directions and a map to save her bitch of a sister.

"That's not all of it, though, is it Mya?" Everyone turned to look at Aurora, surprised by her comment.

"Oh, you are good, Miss Evans. I left that part out to see if you were as good as Ralph hoped you would be." Huh, how the hell did Ralph Knox know about Aurora and her gifts? He never met her.

"How did Ryan's dad know about me?"

"That I honestly don't know. Ralph never disclosed that information. He knew Ryan would cross paths with you somehow. I used to think that Ralph was a seer himself."

"Are you going to tell them, or should I?" Mya smiled at Aurora; clearly Mya was fond of Aurora's abilities.

"I'm sorry, Ryan." Mya took a deep breath and looked Ryan directly in the eyes. I could see from the look on Mya's face she was finding it hard to disclose her news to Ryan. "Stevie accepted the darkness fully into her about three days ago when she held a ceremony on the mountain of our ancestors." Both Alex and Chase gasped; Ryan looked to both her cousins, confused. "Your sister ruled that the coven must fight in the upcoming war." Fuck, now the vampires had the witches on their side.

"How the hell did she do it? There is no way Gregory would have let her accept the throne on the mountain in front of the ancestors. The elders wouldn't have allowed it either! They know Ryan exists now!"

"I am sorry, Alex—Gregory is dead. Stevie was able to complete the ceremony after she murdered him. She took a loved one from each of the elders to force them into aiding her crusade."

What the fuck has that crazy bitch done? I had known Gregory. He was a wise man and an elder. He guarded the mountain path to ensure that no one could access the power of the ancestors without elder approval. Alex and Chase both seem shattered. They turned their backs on their coven to help Ryan and now there coven members were being killed at the hands of their cousin.

"Stevie will answer for her crimes! Blood must have blood!" I have never heard so much venom and hatred come from Alex, there was no coming back for Stevie in his eyes.

"Alex, please, Stevie is sick, she needs our help." Ryan had tears trailing down her face, pleading with her cousins to understand and help her save her sister. Judging by the look on both the guys faces, they wouldn't spit on Stevie if she were on fire.

"She killed an elder, Ryan! A fucking elder. Gregory was a defenseless old man, and she fucking killed him. I am sorry, Ryan, but she has murdered a coven elder and taken our elders' loved ones hostage. It is the Knox coven way, cousin—blood must have blood." Ryan broke out into sobs at Chase's harsh words, and Dom wrapped an arm around her and rubbed his hand up and down her arm, trying to soothe her.

CHAPTER 31

Ryan

I was sobbing into Dom's chest, and I didn't care that the others were watching me breakdown.

"I am sorry, Ryan, but Chase is right. Even if you do save your sister, she will need to answer for the crimes she has committed." I couldn't look at Mya, I know it wasn't her fault, but I was banking on her being the one to help me save my sister. Instead she told the whole room that my sister was pretty much doomed.

"Hang on—our dad is one of the elders, Mya." I turned to look at Alex, wondering what he was getting at, and then it hit me.

"I'm sorry, Alex, I don't know where your mother is. She was taken with the rest of the elders loved ones."

"No! My parents are back in New Zealand." Chase was grasping at straws now.

"Stevie called all coven members back to Wonder Lake the day you, Alex, and Ryan fled. Your parents came as soon as they heard you and Alex went rogue."

"Where is our father, Mya?" Mya dropped her gaze to her

hands in her lap, and I had a sinking feeling her answer was about to hurt my cousins.

"All elders are being held at Randall Cane's mansion. Stevie made sure that she had a get-out-of-jail-free card before she came here to meet Ryan." Alex jumped to his feet and started pacing. Chase did the same and then punched a hole in the wall, screaming. My sister was always one step ahead of us. She had a backup plan in case something went wrong, and that's why she wasn't pissed or angry that she was held in a cell—she knew she wouldn't be stuck in there for long.

"I will fucking kill her!" Chase was glowing purple and his whole body was vibrating with rage.

"Chase, you need to calm down, we will get Mom and Dad back, brother. I swear." Alex was trying to reassure Chase and help him calm down. Chase was taking deep breaths, trying to control his rage.

"How do we get the elders back, Mya?" It was the first time Jackson had spoken since the start of this powwow.

"You need to return Stevie to Randall Cane tomorrow evening at the wedding."

"Evening? The wedding is happening at noon tomorrow." Nico took the words right out of my mouth.

"No, brother, the wedding will happen at night so the vampire king can bring his soldiers with him. Now that Kai and I are no longer with him, he has no fae blood to feed his men." That slimy fucking bastard.

"We played right into his hands. My sister was a distraction. He knew you wouldn't let her go, Nico, he even banked on it. That's why Stevie never fought back. She wanted to be captured so that we would have to change the time of the wedding and play by their rules." Everyone started talking at once, trying to make a plan on how we proceed. I was still stuck on the fact that Stevie knew we would capture her and that Mya would be here to tell us. I jumped to my feet and yelled.

"Everyone shut up!" Silence fell, and I turned my attention to Mya. "How did my sister know that we would come for you?" I know my dad said I could trust her, but something wasn't right.

"Because I told her you would come for me" I recoiled at her admission.

"You sold us out!" I was going to wring her fucking neck.

"It's not what you think, Miss Knox, I swear."

"You have no fucking idea what I am thinking! My father told me I could trust you, and yet you sit here telling us that you are the one who told my sister that we would come for you. How did you know, Mya, and don't fucking lie to me!" I must admit I respected her more when she stood and came to stand directly in front of me, never breaking eye contact. What she said next had me staring at my cousins for confirmation.

"I am a witch, but I am also blessed with the power to see into the future. I saw you coming for me months ago." My cousins looked as shocked as me.

"The Knox coven has no seers, Mya."

"Yes, Alex, they do. I am the only seer, and no one knows of my ability aside from the elders and Ralph Knox." I stumbled backward and plonked down next to Dom, and Mya reclaimed her seat. She was looking at me, waiting for me to piece it all together, but when I did, I wish I hadn't. Sorrow filled me, he knew what was coming.

"My father knew he was going to die, didn't he? You saw it?" I could see the pity in her eyes, telling me all I needed to know.

"Yes, that is why he made sure all his affairs were in order and that the coven knew of the crowning of the new queen. The Knox coven knows of your existence and that you are the true queen. That is why Gregory and the elders forbade your sister from claiming the throne on the mountain of the ancestors."

"Stevie knew, didn't she? That's why she made sure I made the trip to Alaska, so I would renounce the throne to her. It was the only way the elders would let her lead, wasn't it?"

"I believe she did know, yes. If you renounced your claim to the throne, the elders would have to let the next heir in line rule the coven." That's why Stevie was uptight and snappy when I first arrived at her home and even after we arrived here. I knew something wasn't right with my sister, I could see it in her eyes when we got here, but I didn't know any better. The darkness inside her is what is driving her need for power, and that's why she hates me. I'm a threat to her power.

"How did I not see this coming?" Aurora murmured. She seemed annoyed that she didn't see this turn of events.

"Because you are too close to this, your feelings are too far involved. You are the most powerful seer to walk the lands, Aurora Evans, do not doubt your ability."

"What happens now?" Melakai asked the million dollar question.

We all sat around for the next few hours and made a plan to change the wedding from noon to the evening and made sure that we notified everyone of the change of plans. I was shocked to learn that Dom's dad would be here for the wedding tomorrow. It would be cool to meet the alpha of the New York pack. I hated that we had to let my sister go, but I couldn't let my love for her cloud my judgment. Others' lives were at risk here. We agreed that after breakfast we would all go and see Stevie and try to get the information we needed out of her. The guys wanted to torture it out of her, but I quickly shot that idea down. The worst part was that Chase and Alex were on board with hurting Stevie.

After leaving Jackson's office, I went straight back to my room. I was exhausted and needed a solid eight hours of sleep.

After finally getting showered and into bed, I laid there staring up at the ceiling thinking about the past few weeks and how my life had changed so much. I went from being unwanted, unloved, and abused to the girl who had her sister and cousins by her side. I thought we would travel the world together and I would finally be happy.

Then arriving in Alaska changed everything. My whole life had been a lie. I wasn't who I thought I was, and my mother wasn't supposed to be the monster that she is now. My dad was killed, my sister was evil and possibly unredeemable, and I had to marry a guy I thought for years was a figment of my imagination. Oh and let's not forget that the other guy I have been fucking in my dreams is real and tricked me into loving him, and is also best friends with the guy I have to marry. My life is a fucking disaster. I let out a long exhale of air and closed my eyes, I needed to clear my mind and get some sleep. Tomorrow was going to be a long as fuck day. If what we discussed tonight is true, as soon as Nico and I made our vows and sealed it with a kiss, the lock he placed on my powers would shatter.

Nico would help me control them and stop me from dying, hopefully.

According to Mya, my powers needed another life force to help stabilize them in the beginning. Nico would hold some of my power until I could control it and then it would return to me.

I felt like Thor and his hammer, *if he should be worthy he will possess the power.* I need to make sure I was worthy! I had to stop my sister, kick Randall's ass, save my aunt and uncle, and as much as I hated to admit it to even myself. I needed to save my mom.

After leaving Jax's office, I made my way back to my room. I knew it would be hard for me to sleep. The words Ryan said to me earlier played over and over in my mind. *"Kai was definitely the better choice and better man."* She was right. Kai was the better man and the better choice. She needed to choose me, though, or this wouldn't work. I *wanted* her to choose me. A thought crossed my mind then. She may not talk to me here, but she was always more compliant in her dreams. I whispered the chant to take me to our dreamland.

I opened my eyes and turned around to see I was near the dock at Lake William—strange. I was sure I chanted to take us to the forest, not this place that she came with Kai.

"You just gonna stand there or?" I turned to the left and saw her sitting on the grass by the edge of the lake. I made my over to her and sat next to her with my legs extended in front of me. She had her long brown hair down and it was blowing slightly in the breeze. She wore the same white summer dress she always wore in her dreams. She wasn't looking at me, though. She was staring straight ahead at the lake. "Why are we here Nico?"

"Because I am a complete ass and I'm sorry." She didn't turn to look at me and didn't say anything for a few moments.

"Am I your hugacko, Nico?" I whipped my head around so fast I heard my neck crack. How the fuck did she know that? She slowly turned her head so she could look me in the eye, but she gave nothing away with her expression.

"Who told you that?"

"A man told me." What the fuck!

"What fucking man?"

"Brown hair, deep green eyes and I think he was a king." She was toying with me, the smartass.

"Your dad told you?" She just nodded and smiled a sad smile. "I can't control who I...it just happens, and I—" She cut off my rambling by placing her index finger on my lips. I was dying to suck that digit into my mouth, and she must have read my mind because she quickly pulled her hand away.

"I'm not mad, Nico, I just don't understand why you didn't tell me. Before you get mad, Dom also told me about me being your hugacko."

If I had any chance of her ever trusting me again, I needed to be honest with her. I also needed to remain calm and not lose my shit over Dom telling her. He was really starting to piss me off with all his meddling.

"Because I didn't want you to feel like you had to choose me." Her features softened at my admission.

"That is the most selfless thing I have ever heard you say, Nico. I appreciate you trying to respect me enough to let me choose, but I must be honest with you as well." My shoulders dropped, and I turned to look out at the lake. She was about to tell me she didn't want me. "Today when I told you Kai was the better man and the better choice, I wasn't lying." Just dig that dagger in deeper, love. "But he isn't the right choice for me, or the better man for me." I swung my gaze back to her, trying to read her meaning.

"What are you saying, love?" She giggled, and by God, if that wasn't the best sound I heard in a long time.

"I'm saying as soon as Kai lifted his control over my emotions, the love I thought I had for him vanished. Don't get me wrong—Kai will always be important to me. I am truly embarrassed to say this, but I fell in love with a guy who I thought was part of my imagination, only to find out that he was real. When I first saw you in the fae realm, I couldn't believe my luck.

"I have loved you for years, Nico, and never in my wildest dreams did I ever think you would be real and that I would get to love you properly. It was never a question of whether or not I would marry you, Nico. I would always choose you."

I sat there, staring into her beautiful hazel eyes with the peculiar yellow ring, utterly speechless. My hugacko loved me back, and that made me swell with happiness. I know we have fought and hurt each other, but she loved me, and that was all that mattered. I was the luckiest son of a bitch.

"I have loved you since the first time I invaded your dreams. When your fae side is unlocked, you will feel the bond as well."

"I think I already feel it, Nico. It's like a string is always pulling me toward you. It's like I can feel where you are before I even see you." Holy shit, that is exactly how the bond works.

"You are an extraordinary being, love." I gripped the back of her neck and pulled her toward me so I could kiss her, and after a moment she pulled back.

"I need you to promise me something, Nico."

"What is it, love?"

"Don't ever break my heart, and don't ever lie to me again, please. It's hard for me to trust people, and I have tried everything to push you away and not let you in, but you are very persistent."

We both chucked at the truth of that, and when our laughter subsided, she looked at me, waiting for my answer.

"I promise I will cherish your heart for the rest of our days, love. I promise to protect you and love you till my dying breath. I have waited over a century for you, Ryan, and I will never let you go. You are my reason for existing. I will never lie to you again. I will come to you and speak to you about any matters that concern you from this day forth."

Tears were trailing down her cheeks, and I pulled her onto my lap so she was straddling me. She pulled my face to hers and kissed me like I was the oxygen she needed to live.

We stayed in the dreamland for hours, fucking and then making love. We both came to the realization that we didn't like slow and calm. We liked hard, deep, and messy sex. She was like a drug that called to me, an addiction that I never wanted to cure. Ryan Knox was my own personal drug. Finally we both agreed we needed to return to our bodies and rest before tomorrow.

"Nico, wait."

"What is it, love?" She started twirling her hair around her finger and wouldn't meet my gaze. I smiled. After everything we had just done, she was embarrassed. I could see the blush on her cheeks.

"Could you...I mean, only if you wanted to, you don't have to—"

"Just ask me, love." I was trying so hard not to laugh at her awkwardness.

"When we get back, can you come to my room and sleep with me?" I couldn't help it—I laughed, and she glared at me.

"You were just sitting on my face not ten minutes ago, telling me to eat your fucking pussy, and then you get shy asking me to sleep next to you." She was blushing so much and glaring daggers at me. "I'm sorry, love, of course I will come sleep with you." As I *started chanting to get us out of the dreamland, I swear I heard muttering about me being a dick face and needing to be punched.*

As soon as I returned to my bedroom, I got up and made my way to Ryan's room. I knocked on her door, and she opened it for me, and we made our way over to her bed and sunk down under the covers, holding each other. I can't wait to go to bed with her every night and hold her like this.

"Goodnight, big guy." I smiled at her nickname for me.

"Goodnight, my love."

Not five minutes later she was sleeping again. I peered down at her and marveled at her beauty. I would never let anyone harm her. I would kill her sister and Randall both if I had to. I would never let anyone hurt her again, and I sure as fuck wouldn't be a gutless coward and stand by and watch this time. She is to be my wife and, one day, the mother to my children. I would die before I ever let any fucker try and take her from me.

CHAPTER 33

Ryan

I felt like I was burning up, I tried to move to get away from the heat without opening my eyes, but I couldn't seem to move. I opened my eyes quickly and looked down to see an arm around my waist and a leg over my thigh, and that's when it hit me—the heat I was feeling was coming from Nico's body. Memories of the night before came flooding back, and I felt the blush heating my cheeks. I admitted that I was in love with Nico last night, and to top it all off, he told me he loved me too, many times, while he was doing unspeakable things to my body.

"I can feel you overthinking, love." I fought the smile that tried to break free. "Go back to sleep. We don't have to be up for a while." But I couldn't go back to sleep; I wanted to explore Nico while I was awake. I turned so we were facing each other. Nico still had his arm wrapped around me and his leg over mine, and his eyes were still shut. I began to run my fingers across his chest and down his arm. "If you keep doing that, love, there will be no sleep happening." This time I did let the smile break free.

Would it be like this every morning when we woke? Me wanting to jump his bones and him holding me like he never wanted to let me go? I was pulled from my thoughts when Nico suddenly had me pinned beneath him. He looked so beautiful first thing in the morning. His jet black hair was tousled from sleep and his violet eyes were burning with hunger, though he wasn't hungry for food— he was hungry for me. I leaned forward to capture his lips, but he pulled back before I could kiss him. I pouted and he chuckled.

"I know we have done things in your dreams, love, but I want our first *real* time together to be as man and wife." This man could melt me with his words. I could already feel the tears threatening to spill from my eyes. "I didn't mean to upset you, love. Of course I have wanted to do this for a long time but I just thought it might be better to wait, till after the wedding." He looked so crestfallen I reached my hand up to stroke his cheek.

"You didn't upset me, big guy, you just surprised me is all. What you just said means a lot to me, and I appreciate you wanting to wait till after we're married." Nico didn't get a chance to reply as my bedroom door opened with a resounding thud when it hit the wall, I jumped and Nico groaned. What is the point of having a fucking door?

"Does locking a fucking door mean nothing these days?" I laughed at Nico's irritation; every time we seemed to be alone someone always seemed to burst in without knocking.

"Well, that is a sight I could have gone my whole life without seeing." Nico quickly scrambled off me and back to his side of the bed at the sound of his sister's voice.

"What the actual fuck, Soph!"

"Sorry, brother but you both need to get ready for breakfast so we can get this meeting with the evil witch over with, and then we need to get Ryan ready for tonight, so chop-chop."

"How did you get in here?"

"I used magic, of course." Right, of course, Sophia didn't even seem like her not knocking was a big deal. What did I have to do around here to get to some sort of privacy? Not wanting to cause a delay or have Sophia just standing there staring at her brother and me, Nico left the room to shower and change and I did the same thing while Sophia waited for me on the chair.

After showering and changing into jeans and a long-sleeved shirt, I grabbed my sweatshirt from my bag and threw it on, trading my faithful Chucks in for my combat boots. It was starting to get really cold here, so I'm guessing winter was approaching. Due to the weather, we decided to hold our wedding in the chapel at the back of Jax's compound instead of outside. After lacing my boots, I turned to tell Sophia that I was ready to go meet the others in the mess hall, but she didn't hear me. I called her name three times before she finally heard me.

"Sorry."

"Is everything okay, Sophia?" I had never seen Sophia so down and dare I say, sad.

"The man that beat and tortured me for seventeen years is coming to watch my brother get married. Of course I'm okay." I flinched at her dry tone; I didn't even think about how Randall being here would affect Sophia. I am such a shitty person.

"If I could have done this wedding without him being present, I would have Sophia, I swear. I hate that man for what he has done to you and Kai. He has my mother and my uncle now. I have to get them back, and when I do, I promise we will take that bastard down." She didn't answer, and my heart hurt for her and what she had gone through at the hands of that monster. We left the room and made our way toward the mess hall, but I had a question to ask her that was burning a hole in my mind since first meeting her. Clearing my throat and steeling my spine, I blurted it out. "Why is there a painting of you hanging in Randall's office?" Sophia never faltered or paused, just continued walking. I didn't think she was going to answer my question, but as the mess hall doors came into sight, she finally did.

"My painting hangs on his wall because Randall Cane believes he is in love with me." My jaw dropped, but she kept on walking as if she'd never said a thing.

After meeting everyone in the mess hall and quickly eating breakfast, we made our way to the cells. We went down in two groups, as the elevator wasn't big enough for us all to go down together. Once we were all safely down and in the cell block, we made our way over to my sister and Tyler's cells. As we rounded the corner, I saw my sister pacing her cell, muttering under her breath like a crazy person. Tyler was sitting on the cot in his cell with his head clasped between his hands.

"Someone looks like they're going a bit stir crazy." I cut my gaze to Dom, warning him to rein it in; now wasn't the time for jokes. I stopped directly outside my sister's cell with Nico on my side.

"I need you to tell me where the hell you put the family members of the elders you have imprisoned at Randall Cane's manor." My sister continued to pace her small cell, but she didn't bother to hide her smile. She loved every minute of having the upper hand.

"If you had just done as you were told and not fucked everything up, none of this would have happened." Great, now she wanted to blame me for all her problems.

"I'm not the one at fault here, Stevie, you are." My sister stopped pacing and turned to face me, I gasped. Her eyes had changed color— they were black. I could see black lines dancing across her face. Mya was right; I was too late to save my sister.

"Oh, don't look so sad, sister, you knew this would happen. I just didn't let you see the real me yesterday. I will kill everyone you hold dear. I will make you watch as I torture and kill them, and then when I am satisfied that you have suffered enough, I will then kill you." I felt the tears start to build, but I wouldn't let my sister see me cry or show her how much her words affected me. I would be strong and fight till my dying breath. The thought of her touching any of my friends or my cousins sent my blood boiling.

"How the fuck does she have access to magic down here?" Jax hissed, and I turned to see what Jax was talking about, but he wasn't looking at Stevie. I followed his gaze and saw my hands glowing blue. I'm guessing no one was supposed to be able to access magic down here, based on Jax's outburst.

"Because she is the only one who can save us from the darkness that lives inside her own sister." I turned to look at Mya, confused at what she was saying.

"Ahhhh, Mya, my trusty advisor." Mya's upper lip pulled back into a snarl. "Don't be like that! We had fun together, didn't we?" Stevie was smiling at Mya like there was a secret between them.

"Go fuck yourself, Your *Majesty*." Stevie laughed and it was a horrible sound, I can't explain it, but it sounded half like a dog bark and someone having a coughing fit. Stevie stopped laughing after a minute and snapped her gaze back to Mya.

"I, Stevie Lee Knox, hereby banish you, Mya Skye, from the Knox coven. You will not be returned to the mountain of the ancestors when you die, and you are forbidden from any and all contact with any Knox coven member." Mya clutched at her chest right above her heart; there was so much pain etched across her face. "Don't worry, though—my sister isn't a member of the coven, and my cousins are now rogues, so you can still speak to them."

"You can't fucking do this to her, Stevie! You will kill her!" I turned my gaze to Chase, who was making his way over to Mya. She was about to collapse before he got to her but Kai caught her and cradled her to his chest. There was an interesting look on his face, but. Alex's outburst pulled me from my thoughts.

"You fucking bitch! You just condemned our whole coven! Why would you do that?"

"Because she didn't tell you the best part, did she?" Everyone was looking between Stevie and Mya, waiting for one of them to speak and fill in the missing piece of the puzzle. "Oh fine, then I'll tell them, shall I, Mya? She must have forgotten to tell you that in order for you to save that murdering bastard's world, you must kill me, dear sister." What the ever loving fuck is she talking about? "The only way for you to beat me is to unlock those precious powers of yours and learn to control them. You will not succeed at this task, sister; I will kill you before you have a chance."

My knees nearly gave out, but Nico wrapped an arm around my waist and pulled me into his side. My sister just admitted that she would kill me and feel no remorse. How am I supposed to deal with that? All I wanted was to save her from this darkness, and she is too far gone. I can see the blackness running through her veins, and her eyes are a soulless pit. How did my sister become this monster? How did my dad let this go on for so long and not try to stop her? I let my tears fall, not from fear of my life but for heartbreak for my sister. Gone was the girl who used to sit on the phone with me and tell me I was going to be okay, and that she loved me more than anything in the world. My best friend is gone; my other half is dead. The person standing in front of me now isn't my sister. The person standing in front of me is a monster.

"I am so sorry, Stevie." I could hear the others murmuring behind me, clearly they were shocked I was apologizing. "Dad should have tried harder to save you. I should have known about all of this supernatural stuff so I could have helped you."

"You truly are fucking dumb." Nico growled in warning beside me. "Dad couldn't fucking save me! He was a gutless bastard."

"Don't fucking talk about him like that! He loved us, Stevie."

"You stupid, naïve bitch! He found the answer to saving me; he just couldn't go through with what he needed to do." I turned to Mya, trying to read her face for any deceit. She was still in Kai's arms but she had a puzzled look on her beautiful face. Clearly my father hadn't told her about this.

"What do you mean, Stevie?"

"*In order to save one from the fate of darkness, you must kill the light it was born with.* To save me, dad had to kill you." I gasped. That can't be true, can it? "He chose you over me! He deserved his death!" My knees did give out this time, and Nico picked me up and cradled me to his chest like Kai had done to Mya.

"We're done here, you will be released in exchange for the elders return. If you do not meet these terms, you will be executed." As soon as Nico finished speaking, he turned and started to walk away, but before we rounded the corner I saw a look of devastation and panic on Tyler's face.

We left the cells and went straight back to Jackson's office. This place was starting to seem like our headquarters. I took the single chair by the window with Ryan still cradled in my arms. I watched as Kai gently deposited Mya on the other single chair. Kai was looking at her with so much confusion etched across his face, why the hell was he confused? He was so different now. I needed to get my head out of my ass and be there for my brother. Ryan started to sit up and try move to the vacant seat next to Jax, but I wasn't having that. I wrapped my arm tightly around her waist and whispered in her ear.

"You're not going anywhere, love." At my words she relaxed back into my chest, and I could tell from the look on her face she was pushing her emotions down and refusing to deal with them. I knew if she tried to deal with what she had just learned now it would break her, and we wouldn't be having a wedding today or saving any elders.

Her cunt of a sister pretty much just admitted to killing their father, and as soon as Ryan registered what her sister was saying, she collapsed. My strong little spitfire was trying so hard to hold it together.

"We are royally fucked, and I feel like we're missing a key piece to this puzzle." Dom was right—something wasn't adding up. Ryan turned slightly in my lap and faced Mya who looked shattered.

"What happened to you back there, Mya?" Mya continued to stare at her lap. Just when I thought she wasn't going to respond, she quietly said,

"Your sister exiled me from my home." I felt Ryan tense.

"I don't understand what that means, I'm sorry."

"What it means, Ryan, is the place I have called home for nearly a century is no longer my home. As the coven queen, she has the right to banish anyone she wants. I can never return to the coven." I hadn't heard of that ever happening before, so this was all news to me. I was also shocked to hear how old she was, I had never known a witch to live this long before. When Ryan gently moved my arm from around her waist I gave her a stern look, but she nodded her head in Mya's direction, and I let her go and comfort the woman that had just lost everything. Ryan walked over to Mya and knelt down in front of her, grasping both her hands in her own.

"I am so sorry for what my sister has done to you, Mya. I can't comprehend the pain you are going through. Just know that we are all here for you, and you will always have a home with me. I will take back the coven from Stevie, and I will make sure you come back to your home."

Mya started shaking her head. She lifted her gaze to Ryan's and I could see the tears in her eyes.

"You will be a great queen, Ryan Knox, both here and in Farrarie. But you cannot undo what has been done."

"What do you mean?"

"What she is saying, Squirt, is once you are banished or exiled from the coven, you cannot come back. Stevie pulled the bonds from Mya that tie her to the Knox coven, and once they are gone, they're gone." I didn't know that's what happened to witches; in my realm, if you are banished, the king can change his mind and bring you back.

"I am so sorry Mya, what my sister did is...." Mya jumped to her feet, causing Ryan to fall on her ass. I stood and so did the others in the room. Mya was fuming and glaring down at Ryan.

"Your sorry does not fix anything! If your father had just done what he should have, none of this would have happened. You and your sister have ruined everything!" Mya rushed out of the room, and I stood there stunned at her outburst. Kai offered Ryan his hand to help her to her feet.

"She didn't mean what she said; she just lost her home and is lashing out." Why the fuck was Kai defending this witch?

"I'm not angry at her, Kai, my heart hurts for her and all that she has lost at the hands of my sister." Ryan looked past Kai to the clock that said it was half past ten and sighed. "The wedding is at eight tonight, and we are running out of time, what the hell do we do?" Aurora spoke before anyone else could.

"We send Tyler back to Randall with a message to release all your coven elders and to find the loved ones your sister has hidden." Is she out of her ever loving fucking mind?

"Rora, your brother is a traitor and can't be trusted." Finally something I can agree on with Alex.

"He will do as he is asked."

"How do you know this for certain?" I asked Aurora.

"Because he will do whatever it takes to ensure his mate's safety." Everyone in the room except for Ryan seemed shocked at Aurora's admission. After a second, Jax started pacing his office.

"That's why my best friend did it, isn't it? He betrayed me because he mated with that psycho bitch." Aurora nodded and Ryan still said nothing—why?

"Love, why don't you seem shocked about your sister being a

werewolf's mate? You do know that a wolf has never mated outside of their race before, right?" Ryan took a deep breath before looking around the room and then settling her gaze on me. I saw the answer before she even said it.

"I knew Stevie was Tyler's mate." Everyone started shouting.

"When?"

"How long have you known?"

"Why didn't you say anything?"

"Silence!" Everyone stopped talking and turned to face me. I guess I wasn't the only one who had hidden things. "How long have you known about this, love?" Ryan squared her shoulders and lifted her head staring directly into my eyes.

"Since the day they arrived here, Tyler told me she was his mate." She has known for a couple of days and still said nothing to anyone?

"Why didn't you say anything, Ry?" I could hear the betrayal in Jackson's voice. Tyler was his beta and his friend. Jackson thought he betrayed him because he liked Stevie, only to find out it was deeper than that.

"Because Tyler asked me not to. I know you will all think I'm crazy, but I believe Tyler is trying to help us stop Stevie. He doesn't want to hurt anyone or seal the fae realm. He just wants to fix my sister. He has been trying to guide her to do the right thing, but the more he pushes the more she pushes him away."

"I knew my brother wouldn't leave me, I just knew it."

"But you knew, as well, didn't you, *mate?*" Jax spat the word *mate* at Aurora like it burned his tongue. She flinched at his cold tone and dropped her gaze to the floor.

"I didn't have a vision, if that's what you're insinuating, Jax. Tyler told me while you were all distracted with Stevie and Mya." You sneaky little devil, Aurora.

"What else did your brother say?" Jackson was being so cold toward Aurora, as if she had betrayed him as well.

"He said that he would help us get the coven elders back and try to help us find their loved ones. He believes Stevie has their loved ones locked in the basement at her cabin."

"He fucking tricked you! He is a liar and a rat bastard, Aurora." Aurora started shaking and began to cry. Dom cut in front of Aurora to block her from Jackson's view. Jax started growling, his eyes turning yellow.

"She may be your mate, brother but you will not fucking speak to her like that again!" Jackson didn't respond. His growl started to intensify and his eyes started to change to his wolfs. "She lost her brother and you lost your friend, do not take your anger out on her for loving her brother! She has done nothing wrong, Jackson." Jax's eye slowly started to return to their normal chocolate brown color, and once he had himself under control, his shoulders sagged. He knew he fucked up.

"Aurora, I'm sorry. I should never have lashed out at you; it's not your fault. My wolf is starting to pick up your faint scent, and it's driving him crazy that he can't fully scent you. It's no excuse, but I'm on edge and so is he. He's jealous that Tyler found his mate." I dropped my head in shame at Jax's quiet admission; I felt like a piece of shit for my hand in helping Aurora conceal herself from him.

"I'm sorry, Jackson, but now isn't the time to deal with us, I want to ask your permission this time, though." Jackson lifted his head and Dom stepped aside to let him see Aurora.

"My permission for what?"

"To let Nico conceal my scent again." Jackson recoiled like Aurora had slapped him. "You need to understand, Jackson. Right now, I need my abilities to help us. As soon as all this is over, I swear we will sit down and talk about this and sort something out." Aurora was pleading with Jackson to understand her logic, and she was right, we needed her seer abilities now more than ever.

Jax looked around for a moment and then his hard, untrusting gaze landed on me. He was contemplating whether or not I would betray him and go behind his back again. I wouldn't, not this time, and plus, if I did, I am ninety-nine percent sure Ryan would hurt my balls.

"I will not do anything without your consent, brother. I swear to you that you have my word. I will not go behind your back again." Jax moved his gaze from me and then turned to Kai and Dom and asked.

"What would you do?"

"I would do what was best for my people; I would want to save the lives of my family and friends first." Dom was so political in his response, Kai was still silent.

"Kai?" At the mention of his name, Kai looked to Jackson and then Ryan, sighing before answering.

"I would claim the love of my life before I had a chance to lose her. There is no guarantee we will all survive this battle, so I would want to claim what is mine and love her while I had the chance." I looked around the room and noticed the three women had tears glistening in their eyes, while the guys stood there mouths hanging open and staring at the huge blond haired, blue-eyed vampire. I think we were all in shock at Kai's confession; I have never heard him talk like this before. Ryan was staring at him in awe, and it made me fidget and feel slightly irritated. She has never looked at *me* like that before. Ryan made her way over to Kai and grasped his hand in hers. I couldn't hold my grunt in even if I tried. She turned to glare at me and then focused her attention back on Kai, who was looking down at her with a look of longing and hurt.

"You will find the one for you, Kai, and when you do, she will be the luckiest woman in the world. You are a beautiful man with a kind heart, and I will always be here for you. The world is a better place with someone like you in it. I love you, Kai." Kai didn't reply, he just continued to stare at her. I needed to break their moment apart stat!

"Okay, so back to Jax and Aurora now. Do you want me to cast that spell?" Everyone in the room turned to glare at me, except for the fucking two warlocks, who started laughing at my expense. I was really getting tired of those bastards.

"You are such a dick, Tink. She is marrying you in like"— Chase looked at his wrist to check the time—"nine hours, and you're still jealous over her talking to Melakai." The fucker had the balls to burst out laughing again and was quickly followed by his brother and Dom. I glared at Dom, the fucking bastard, who's side was he fucking on?

CHAPTER 35

After the guys got their laughter under control, we all sat down and agreed to let Tyler go back to Randall with our message. Nico and Dom were going to tell him the terms and what was at stake. I didn't want to go and see my sister again. I couldn't. If I did, I knew I would have to deal with what she told me, and right now I didn't have any time for a breakdown. We needed to wrap up this meeting, as Sophia said I had a lot to do before my wedding this evening. I had no idea what she meant, but she was adamant that I had a shit load to do. Who was I to argue with the princess of Farrarie and my future sister in law? I was pulled from my thoughts when Jax spoke.

"Okay, if this is what you want, Aurora, I will do it for you." Jax and Aurora were staring at each other, and it felt intimate. Aurora seemed shocked that Jax would agree to her request.

"Thank you, Jackson."

"I have one condition though." Aurora took a deep breath and then nodded to Jackson. "I want you to move into the room next to mine. You being near will calm my wolf." Aurora tilted her head to the side, clearly at a loss.

"But your wolf was fine before."

"My wolf and I didn't know you were our mate then. This spell will mask your scent so my wolf won't claim you, but it won't stop him from knowing you're his mate. Grant me this one thing, Aurora, and I will agree to the spell. I will hold you to your promise, though, that as soon as all this is over you and I will talk."

Aurora agreed and said she would move into the room next to Jax's first thing tomorrow. Nico cast the spell soon after Jax agreed. We all said our goodbyes and filed out of the room. I was walking down the hall with Sophia and Aurora on either side of me when Nico called out.

"Can I talk to you for a moment please, love?" I turned back to tell the girls that I would meet them in my room shortly.

"What's wrong, big man?" He seemed nervous and kept moving from foot to foot, he put his hands in the pockets of his jeans and looked down. His hair fell forward and hung over his face so I couldn't see his eyes.

"I just want to make sure that...you know...you're okay with...and that you were sure?" What the hell was he saying?

"I don't understand what you're asking me, big guy." I was keeping my tone light so it would help put him at ease. He blew out a long exhale and then lifted his head so I could see his eyes.

"Are you sure you want to marry me?" Oh my God, I swear to fucking whoever was listening I just swooned so fucking hard for this man. I grabbed his face between both my hands and pulled his face down to mine so I could kiss him. The kiss was slow and unhurried. I was trying to tell him with this kiss that I was sure, and I was ready to marry him. I was literally marrying my soulmate, and tonight, when my powers were free, my soul would merge with his as his hugacko. I pulled back and looked him in the eyes and smiled.

"Of course I'm sure, big guy. I want to do this with you. We're gonna fight and we're both going to piss each other off while we get to know each other better, but we'll make it through, I promise." He smiled his signature panty-melting smile and pecked me on my lips again.

"You better go, then, before my sister comes looking for you." I gave him another kiss and quickly made my way to my room. As soon as I opened the door, I wished I had stayed in Jackson's office. My room was full of beauty products that were scattered everywhere; there were at least four dress racks that held different colors and types of dresses. There were flower arrangements all over the room, and Sophia and Aurora were sorting through the dresses. When I closed the door behind me, they both looked up, and Aurora squealed.

"Ryan! Come on you have to choose your dress and what flowers you want, and we need to do your hair and makeup." Aurora was talking so fast I could barely make out what she was saying, I think she was more excited about the wedding than Nico and me.

I didn't get a chance to answer, as someone knocked on my door, thank God. I quickly turned and went to answer the door to buy myself some time before I was subjected to trying on dresses. I opened the door and standing on the other side was Mya. She looked so remorseful. I stepped aside and invited her in, her eyes were as wide as dinner plates when she saw my room and all the stuff scattered everywhere.

"Sorry, you're busy, I'll go." I put my arm out to stop her and said.

"Please stay." We stared at each other for a long moment and that look alone conveyed everything we hadn't said, that she was sorry for what she said and she didn't mean it. I was saying I was sorry for everything my sister had done to her. We were both wiping the moisture from under our eyes and then hugged, letting bygones be bygones.

After leaving Ryan and making sure she wanted to go ahead with the wedding, I made my way out to the shack to meet Dom. When I arrived, Dom wasn't alone—Jax and Kai stood beside him.

"I thought you two had other plans that you needed to deal with?" None of them answered me, they just turned and opened the door. Alrighty then, I guess we're not talking now. Once we made it to the bottom, we all exited the elevator and made our way toward the back cells that housed Stevie and Tyler. As soon as we rounded the corner, the evil bitch was standing in front of her cell with her arms hanging out of the bars. Jax growled, and she smiled. They may be twins, but they were nothing alike. Ryan was kind and caring, and Stevie was dark and power hungry. She didn't care if she hurt people.

"Back on your own, are we, boys?" I ignored the bitch; I had nothing to say to that vile murdering waste of space. Tyler was standing at the front of his cell, looking between the four of us and Stevie, trying to figure out what we had planned.

"Why didn't you tell me, Tyler?" Tyler looked to Jax, and I saw a crack in the mask Tyler was wearing; he didn't want to hurt Jackson. Ryan and Aurora were right—Tyler hated what he was doing but wouldn't give up his mate.

"Because you didn't need to know. You chose your side and I chose mine!" Tyler's words were lacking the bite you would expect from someone who hated you. Jax didn't respond, just nodded his head and pulled the key for Tyler's cell from his pocket.

"You fucking touch him and I will kill you! I will rip your bride apart." Fuck it, I spun around and pulled every bit of energy I had in me and released an energy ball that hit her in the chest and sent her crashing into the back wall of her cell. Holy shit, I never expected it to work. How the fuck did I do that?

"How the fuck did you do that down here, Nico?" I turned and just shook my head; I had no idea how I had access to my magic down here. Was Ryan's magic already starting to merge with mine?

"You fucking prick! I'll rip your fucking head off!" Tyler was angry and spewing insult after insult at me. Jax opened the cell door and he and Kai wrestled Tyler's arms behind his back and attached some cuffs that were iron infused with silver, and led him out the cell toward the elevator. He was fighting against their hold, trying to check on Stevie.

"If you stopped fucking yelling and struggling, you would hear her heart is still fucking beating!" Tyler stopped struggling against Kai and Jax's hold and listened like Jackson told him, and after a moment he relaxed in their grip and continued to walk to the elevator without a fuss.

Once at the top, we walked around the compound to the front of the property, garnering dirty looks and insults from pack members. Their insults and dirty looks were for Tyler, not us. They saw him as a rat and traitor. They didn't know he left to be with his mate. Tyler hung his head in shame; he knew his pack hated him right now.

"Keep your head up and don't let them see you as weak." Tyler turned to look at Jax, who refused to meet his beta's gaze. Tyler held his head high and straightened to his full height. Insults were still being thrown his way, but he didn't falter, and continued to walk with his head held high. Jackson was a great alpha. As soon as we reached the front of the property, we made our way into the woods, away from prying eyes. We continued to walk until Jax told us we were far enough away from his pack that they couldn't hear or see us. Jax released his hold on Tyler and stepped in front of him.

"We are releasing you to return to Randall, to pass on a message." Tyler nodded his head. "You will tell him that he is to bring the Knox coven elders with him tonight to the ceremony; he obviously knows we changed the time of the wedding to suit his fucking needs." Tyler just nodded again.

"If you betray us and try something stupid, Tyler, we will kill your mate." At Dom's declaration, Tyler turned and glared at him, growling low in his throat. "You obviously know this trail well, pup. You will pass the cabin where you believe your mate has imprisoned the elders' loved ones. You will set them free before returning to Randall." Tyler started shaking his head.

"She will never forgive me if I do this. She knew you would send me back to Randall to free the elders, but she will hate me for going against her and freeing her bargaining chips. If they're even in the cabin." The four of us shared a look between ourselves. We didn't care about Stevie and Tyler's relationship; that was his problem. We did, however, care about the wellbeing of innocent coven members. Jax pulled a burner phone from his pocket and placed it in Tyler's front pocket.

"When you reach the cabin, and *if* they are there, you are to set them free and then call me. After that, you go to Randall and bring the elders back tonight. The ceremony starts at eight, so don't be late." Jax uncuffed Tyler and sent him on his way, and we stood there and watched until he disappeared from view.

"Do you think he will actually go through with it?" Dom voiced the question we were all wondering.

"Yes, because the alpha of all alphas is his sister's mate." We all spun around to see who spoke. I knew he was coming, but it was still a shock to see him after so many years. "It's good to see you all back together again."

"It's good to see you too, sir." Jackson was such a kiss ass. Dom and I rolled our eyes.

"It's good to see you too, Dad," said Dom, as the two men hugged. He pulled back and looked at his son.

"Would you look at that, my baby boy has gone and grown up on me."

Kai, Jax, and I laughed at Dom's dad's teasing. Dom got his quick wit and smartass mouth from his father. Ian Silver was a beast of a man, standing well over six feet tall, with broad shoulders. He had tanned skin like Dom and the same silver-blond hair. They could have been twins, except Dom had violet eyes, the same as his mother's, and Ian had green eyes. We don't speak about Dom's mom; that was a touchy subject still nearly seventy years later. Dom pushed his dad away and started to try and fix his hair since his dad ruffled it. The rest of us shook hands and welcomed Mr. Silver back to the homeland. Jax may be the alpha of all alphas but we all respected Mr. Silver, he is wise and kind and also helped Jax as much as Ralph Knox did when he first took over being Alpha of his pack.

"What did you mean, sir, when you said he would do it because of his sister?"

"He will do as you ask, Jackson, because even though the witch is his mate, he still loves and cares for his sister. He won't risk your wrath against his sister; he would rather take the punishment his mate gives him than hurt Aurora."

"How did you know Aurora was my mate, sir?"

"My word, you boys should know by now that Dominic can't keep his mouth shut about any gossip." We all turned to Dom, who refused to meet our stares and was focusing his attention on his nails like they were the most interesting thing in the world.

"Dominic!" Dom sighed and then finally turned to Jax and shrugged his shoulders.

"What do you want me to say, Jax? It was fucking hard! I tried, I swear I did, but then dad asked if I knew anything new and then it poured out like diarrhea after a night on the booze." We all busted out laughing at Dom; he could never keep a fucking secret. If your life depended on a secret, don't ever tell Dom. You would be dead within minutes. "Stop fucking laughing at me!"

"Dominic, language!" We all laughed harder at Mr. Silver telling his son off. Oh he's going to be in for a treat, Dom had the mouth of a sailor these days.

CHAPTER 37

Ryan

Aurora had run me a bath and told me I had to soak in the oils she had put in and wash my hair and shave. I wasn't going to argue; I had been dying to try out the massive claw foot tub in my bathroom but hadn't found the time to do so. After soaking for a bit and washing my hair with the amazing passionfruit and mango shampoo and conditioner Aurora had given me, I shaved everywhere. Sophia insisted that I should get waxed, but I flat out refused to let anyone wax my coochie. After my bath, I wrapped myself in my robe and put my hair up in a towel. I was now sitting on a chair that wasn't in my room before, with Aurora putting cream on my face that she swore would make me shimmer in the light of the moon.

She moved on to doing my hair and makeup next. I wasn't allowed to look until I was done and in my dress. The dress I picked out is a dress I would never have ever thought I would wear, but I just knew that Nico would love it.

My fingernails and toenails were waiting to be painted.

I felt bad Aurora was doing all this work while I sat here.

Sophia and Mya were sitting on the couch, watching Aurora do her thing with my hair and face, neither of them had done anything aside from drink the champagne that was being brought in. Every time they neared the bottom of the bottle, someone would knock and bring in a fresh bottle.

After hours of sitting here in the same spot, my ass started to protest and go numb. I was also nearing the end of my patience. I had been plucked and shaved, and my hair had been pulled every which way. My face felt like it was covered in mud. My fingernails and toenails had been scrubbed and soaked then scrubbed again. I wasn't a girly girl, so having to endure all of this for hours might be some other woman's idea of fun, but for me it was pure fucking hell. Sophia and Mya kept giggling every time they saw the look on my face. They were enjoying my discomfort, the assholes.

"Okay, Ry, I'm nearly done, and then you can put your dress on."

"Aurora, it's still early. Can't I wait till just before the wedding?"

"What are you talking about, Ryan?"

"What's the time, Aurora?"

"Ryan, it's seven. You get married in an hour." What the actual fuck? Where has the time gone? I started to panic. Holy fuck, I'm getting married, and I'm only eighteen. I'm going to be a teen bride. What's next, kids? I'm not ready to be a mom; I haven't even lived yet. Fuck, and I will have to move to Farrarie with Nico? What about the coven? What about my cousins? I started to hyperventilate; Aurora placed both her hands on my shoulders, trying to get me to look at her. My vision was going foggy.

"Ryan!" I looked up to see Sophia and Mya were now standing next to Aurora. "Snap out of it, now! You're going to blow this whole fucking room up otherwise." I looked down to see I was glowing; I couldn't get enough air into my lungs. All I could hear was my own heartbeat in my ears, like a drum.

Everything else was white noise. I was being shaken, and I managed to lift my gaze and then my eyes locked onto beautiful violet eyes.

"I need you to calm down, love, before your groom breaks down your door. I don't think Jax wants to replace that door for a third time." I couldn't communicate, no words were coming out of my mouth. "It's okay, love. Deep breaths. I guess you're probably freaking out about getting married, huh?"

I nodded my head, still struggling to calm myself. "Will it help you to know that my dad is here, and I am constantly being yelled at for swearing, and if I make a crude remark the old bastard just slaps me up the back of the head?" Listening to Dom was helping me get my breathing under control. He kept talking about mundane things to try and distract me, and it worked. After a few minutes I could finally breathe properly and the pounding in my ears had stopped.

"Thank you, Dom."

"How about you thank me by telling me what had you so freaked out?" I was a bit embarrassed to admit what set me off.

"It just hit me that I'm getting married, and I'm only eighteen. I'm going to be a teen bride like something out of an afterschool special! Will Nico expect babies from me straight away? I don't want kids! I would be a terrible mother, and I'm going to have to move to Farrarie. What about my coven? What about my cousins?"

"Wow, hang on a second love and take a deep breath for me." I did as I was asked and took a deep breath. "Okay let's start from the beginning. Yes, you are getting married and no Nico doesn't expect babies from you immediately. You are not your mother, love, and you will be a great mother when the time does come. Yes, Nico will have to return to Farrarie. He is the king, after all. I'm sure you and Nico could work out together what happens with your coven. Nico doesn't expect you to give everything up, love, him being here as long as he has shows me how much you mean to him. He has never stayed away from his realm longer than a full day. He is choosing you over his people and over his duty to those people. He would never force you to do anything you didn't want to do." I could feel the tears building behind my eyes, and I quickly tried to blink them away for fear of ruining my makeup. Dom was right; Nico was a good man, and he understood me. We could work all this out together, I looked up to see my cousins enter the room. "Now why don't you tell me the *real* reason you freaked out?" How did he know? I felt my bottom lip start to tremble; I took a few deep breaths and then told him the true reason I had a panic attack.

"My dad isn't here to walk me down the aisle. He isn't here to give me away and tell me how beautiful I look." A tear snaked its way down my cheek, and I quickly brushed it away. Dom placed his hand under my chin, lifting my head so he could look me in the eyes.

"I never want to give you away, but I will, if that is what you truly want. You look more beautiful than I have ever seen, Ry. If you will accept us, Alex and I would both love to walk you down the aisle. Uncle Ralph may not be here physically, but he is here in our hearts and in spirit, Ry." Fuck, hearing Chase's speech broke the dam; tears were rolling down my face. I couldn't talk past the lump in my throat, so I just nodded my head and quickly pushed past Dom to hug both my cousins. I would be so fucking lost without them; they have been here for me through all of this shit.

"Okay, I'm sorry, but all you boys have to leave now so I can re-do her makeup and get her in her dress. We will meet you there, Chase and Alex, please be at the front of the chapel by five to eight." Alex and Chase gave me a hug before they left, Dom made his way toward the door but stopped and turned back to me and placed a small kiss on my cheek.

"You look beautiful, love. Nico is a very lucky man to have such a fierce and loving woman by his side."

"Right, come on, were running out of time." Aurora was barking orders at Sophia and Mya to hurry up and change while she touched up my makeup and helped me into my dress. I could do this. I *want* to do this. I mean, who can actually say they get to marry their dream man?

I still wanted to throttle my three best friends. Jax and Kai had held me back while Dom went to comfort Ryan. We were all sharing a drink with Dom's dad after we got ready, when I felt a sharp pain in my chest and knew straight away something was wrong with Ryan. I ran from the room with my friends hot on my tail, and right as I was about to open her bedroom door, I was tackled to the ground by Melakai. He and Jax restrained me while Dom went in. Mr. Silver was telling me to calm down and trust Dom. I did trust Dom, with my life, but Ryan needed me. I wanted to blast these bastards for holding me back, but I knew even if I did get them off, Mr. Silver would still be there blocking the door, and I could never hurt him, I respected him too much.

Mr. Silver told me it was bad luck for me to see my bride before the wedding, so I had to calm down and let Dom handle this. When Dom finally left her room after her cousins, I hit him straight across the jaw. He deserved way worse. The bastard had the cheek to just laugh and rub his jaw.

After pulling myself together and calming myself down, we made our way to the chapel, which was out the back of Jax's compound. It wasn't a huge chapel, but it was big enough to seat a hundred people. By the time we got there, it was nearly seven-thirty. Just as we started to walk up the stairs, I felt the hairs on the back of my neck stand up and spun around quickly. Walking straight toward us was none other than the bastard Randall Cane. He walked with his head held high. He was a short, plump bastard. He wore a suit and tie like us, except his suit was blood red. How fucking cliché.

His blond hair was slicked back, and he was surrounded by his soldiers. It is an ancient law that when a member of royalty from any of the races marry, all the heads of the leading covens and clans must attend. We were not allowed to harm each other at these events; it was forbidden. For the first time in my life I wanted to break that law, but if I did, the elders from each clan would make sure that I paid the price for my insubordination. King or not, no one was above the elders.

What was the point of having elders, when they never fucking did anything anyway? Each supernatural race had elders; they were the ones who upheld our laws. They wouldn't intervene now, though, even with Randall trying to kill my fucking realm. Stevie might have been onto something with manipulating her elders to do as she said. Randall was standing on the bottom step below us. He wasn't looking at me, though—his gaze was fixed on Kai. It felt great to see the shock on this old twat's face: he thought he killed his greatest weapon, yet here Kai stood.

"You're supposed to be dead." Kai smiled an evil smile; he had no emotion displayed on his face other than his hatred for Randall. Kai made his way back down the stairs to stand in front of Randall. Randall's soldiers moved to block Kai, but Dom quickly erected a shield to hold them back. Randall's eyes were darting everywhere, trying to find an escape route, and found there wasn't one. He was fucking pathetic. Kai wouldn't harm him. He knew the rules, and he also knew we needed him alive for the exchange of Stevie and the Knox coven elders.

"Before this night is done, I will fucking kill you! Fuck the elders' laws...I would gladly take their punishment just to see you fall." You didn't even need to be a shifter to hear how loudly Randall gulped. Kai turned and made his way up the stairs, continuing into the chapel to take his place.

"Put him on a leash, king." I smiled. Kai had rattled Randall and made him flustered. Before Dom dropped the shield holding Randall's minions back, I spoke.

"Melakai will never be on a leash now that he is free of your vile ass. You ever come for my brother or try in any way to harm him, and I will burn your fucking mansion to the ground with you in it, you gutless leech." Dom dropped his shield and he and Jax followed me inside to take our places at the front of the podium. Jax, Kai, and Dom were my witnesses.

After talking among ourselves for a bit, the minister announced we were five minutes out from the ceremony starting. I turned to thank the minister and stopped when I saw who the minister was.

"What are you doing here, Gabriel?" The old man smiled at my surprise.

"Did you really think I would let anyone else marry you?" Gabriel was the leader of the fae elders and my father's best friend; he married my mother and father.

"I tried to get in contact with you to see if you could do the ceremony, but Larick said he couldn't find you."

"I was in the Southern kingdom on elder business, but as soon as I heard you were to be married, I dropped everything and came. Thanks to you blocking all the portals, it was a bloody hard job getting here. I had to sneak through with Larick and Maverick and some of the other elders." I smiled at his devious ways. As old as he was, Gabriel was still a mischievous shit. "Are you ready, my boy?" I didn't hesitate to answer.

"I am beyond ready."

As soon as I finished speaking, music began to play and everyone quieted down and took their seats. A minute later, the doors opened, and Mya walked through carrying a bouquet of purple flowers. She wore an off the shoulder purple dress that matched the flowers she held. She made her way down the aisle and stopped on the opposite side from where we stood. Sophia walked through the doors next, her beautiful curly black hair up in an intricate bun.

She didn't have access to her fae magic, but she had the violet eyes of a fae. She wore a yellow dress that matched her flowers, and as she was approaching the front row, her step faltered when she saw Randall there smiling at her. She didn't move, she just stood there staring.

Dom raced over and placed his hand on her back, guiding her to her spot on the other side of the church. I tried to catch her gaze, but she wouldn't look at me, Dom whispered something in her ear that had her nodding and then he returned to his place behind me. The next to walk through was Aurora; she wore a blue dress that matched her eyes and the flowers she held, and she was searching the pews for someone, but I didn't know who. When she reached the end of the aisle, she deflated slightly, clearly annoyed whoever she was looking for wasn't here. Strange.

The music changed, and the small band in the back started a slow song. My eyes were fixed on the double doors, my breath stuck in my throat. The anticipation of seeing Ryan was killing me. If she didn't hurry her pretty little ass up and walk through those doors soon, I would go and get her myself.

My breath caught in my throat as soon as she came into view. Her long brown hair was done up in some sort of braid-bun, with little blue wildflowers placed throughout her hair. The dress she was wearing hugged her luscious curves in all the right ways. It was low cut in the front, and even I could tell from this distance that there was no way she could wear a bra with that dress. The sleeves hung off her shoulders, and the dress flowed behind her. The dress was an ivory color and had an intricate lace overlay. When she stopped at the start of the aisle, it was then that I noticed her cousins were on either side of her. Her gaze was locked on mine, and she was begging me with her eyes to give her strength to do this. I gave her a small nod and saw her exhale.

CHAPTER 39

Ryan

Standing at the top of the aisle, looking at Nico in his suit, caused me to pause. He looked so handsome, with his hair slicked back, and his suit fit him like a glove. I was scared. I looked to him, hoping he could see me begging him with my eyes to loan me some of his strength. When I saw his small nod, I released the breath I was holding.

Looking around the small chapel, I saw so many people sitting in the pews that I didn't know. I would give anything to have my dad and sister here with me. There were thousands of candles lit throughout the chapel, and there were wildflowers hanging from the pews and the chandelier. It was beautiful. It felt like we were in the woods, and that is what I really wanted —to be married outside—but due to the weather and it being too open in case of an attack, we moved the wedding to the chapel.

"Deep breath, Squirt. You can do this." I looked to Alex and nodded, placing my arm through his. I then turned to look at Chase, who was looking down at me.

"If you want to bail and not marry the fairy, I'm all for that too." At the sound of someone growling, I quickly looked to the front of the chapel and saw Nico, Jax, Kai, and Dom glaring at my cousin. Okay, I guess the growl was one of them.

"Chase, I want to do this." He smiled and kissed my hand before I placed my arm in his.

"That's all I needed to hear, Ry."

We made our way down the aisle. I refused to look at the people here. I focused all my attention on Nico. Seeing him standing there, waiting for me, gave me the strength I needed to make it down this aisle and stand before all of these people. Nico made me feel like I could do anything. I pulled my gaze from Nico's when the minister cleared his throat.

"Who gives this woman to this man?" The minister was looking at my cousins with kind eyes; he seemed like a nice man, and clearly he was a fae, as his eyes were violet.

"I, Alexander Knox, from the Knox coven, give Ryan Knox to Nicholas Stone." I was so emotional; I wanted to burst into tears at how proud Alex sounded.

"And I, Chase Knox, also from the Knox coven, give Ryan Knox to Nicholas Stone. Who I know will treat her well and love her like she deserves." I looked to Chase, shocked, and then back to Nico, expecting to see anger on his face, but instead all I saw was respect. He respected Chase for protecting me.

"You have my word, Mr. Knox, that I will love her till the day I die and treat her like the queen she already is." Oh my God, I swooned, and the crowd murmured their hushed approval. The minister motioned for Nico to take my hand, which he did, and Alex and Chase took their seats in the front pew. I couldn't focus on anything else except for Nico. I was one lucky woman. Even with heels on, I had to crane my neck back to look him in the eye.

"We are gathered here today to celebrate the union of the king of Farrarie, Nicholas Stone, and the queen of the Knox coven, Ryan Knox." I heard murmurs around the chapel and grunts of disagreement at my title. I dropped my gaze only for Nico to put his finger under my chin and lift my gaze back to him.

"Never look down, love. You *are* queen, and they will fucking know it soon enough." Nico spoke quietly so only I could hear. I gave him a stiff nod and continued to hold my head high as the minister continued to speak. I was shaken from my daze when the minister called Nico's name. I looked at Nico, confused, but he just smiled and winked at me.

"You can read your vows now, son." What? Nico wrote his own vows? Shit! I didn't write anything for him. Why am I always awkward like this?

"Shhhh, love, it's fine." Clearing his throat, he spoke louder so everyone could hear.

"Ryan Knox, you are an amazing, talented, and strong woman with a heart of gold and the purest soul I have ever encountered. I met you by chance many years ago. I didn't know then that you were to grow and become my hugacko." Murmurs broke out across the chapel again, people clearly shocked at Nico's admission. Judging from the smile on his face, that is what he was aiming for.

"You, Ryan, are my better half. You are the other half to my soul. Without you, there is no me. I promise to love you from this day forth, and I promise to stand by your side and fight beside you through every battle. I promise to adore you till the end of time. Ryan Knox, I have been in love with you since the first time I came to you in your dreams two years ago, and I am the happiest and luckiest man alive to be able to be standing here in front of you today. I cannot wait to be able to call you my wife. I love you, Ry." I was crying. I could feel the tears rolling down my cheeks. I couldn't wait any longer; I stood on my tiptoes and pulled his face down to mine and kissed him. After a minute, I heard someone clearing their throat.

"Cut it out, you two, we haven't gotten to that part yet" I pulled away from Nico to see Dom grinning at me and wiggling his eyebrows. I couldn't help but blush.

"Okay, well, let's get to that part already, shall we?" I chuckled at the minister and so did a few others. "Do you, Ryan Knox, take this man to be your husband?"

"I do."

"And do you, Nicholas Stone, take this woman to be your wife?"

"I do."

"Then by the powers invested in me by the elder council in Farrarie, I now pronounce you husband and wife. Nico, you may *now* kiss your bride." Nico leaned down to place his lips on mine, but I felt a sharp pain in my chest and gasped.

"What is it, love?" I couldn't talk past the pain, it was excruciating. I felt like someone was ripping my chest open.

"Everyone out now!"

"Get the fuck out!"

I didn't know who was shouting and telling everyone to get out. I was too consumed by the pain in my chest. As another wave of pain hit, my knees gave out, and I landed with a thud. Nico quickly grabbed my head before it could hit the stairs. The pain was getting worse. I screamed out as another wave of pain ripped through me.

"It's the bounds on her power. Dom, put up a force field to minimize any damage now. Alex, Chase—I need you both to help him maintain the blast. There are too many people outside if this goes sideways; they will get hurt." I closed my eyes, trying to focus on not screaming. My body started to feel hot. I could feel myself getting hotter and hotter, from the tips of my toes to the tips of my fingers.

"What do we do?"

"I have no idea."

I couldn't hold it in anymore. I screamed out, in agony. I felt like I was being burned alive.

I was clawing at my dress, trying to rip it off. I needed to get all my clothes off to try cool myself down, but I couldn't focus.

My head was pounding and felt like it was going to burst any minute. Fuck, right now I would welcome death if it would just make this pain stop. My veins felt like they were filled with liquid lava, and I couldn't hear or see anything now. It was all just fire and fury.

"What do we do?"

"We have to help her!"

"I don't fucking know how to help her!" I shouted.

"We need to figure it out and fast, because she is dying!"

"You don't think I fucking know that, Jackson?"

I was scared. I never got scared, but seeing the woman I love writhing in pain in front of me and screaming out to make it stop, begging for me to help her? I felt useless. I didn't know how to make it stop, and I didn't know how to take the pain away.

"Nico! It hurts, it hurts so fucking much!" She was starting to glow blue, and a blue mist started coating her body, starting at her feet and making its way up slowly. Out of the corner of my eye, I saw Aurora drop to her knees; I turned to her, prepared to try and catch her if she fell, but Jackson stopped me.

"Don't touch her! She's having a vision." Sure enough, Aurora's eyes were white. This vision didn't last long, maybe a minute, if that. As soon as Aurora's eyes turned back to their normal color, she turned to me.

"Kiss her, Nico!"

"What?"

"You never sealed the exchange after the vows; she kissed you before them. You must kiss her and accept her power into you." Fuck! Right now I would try anything. I leaned my head down toward hers and whispered.

"I'm gonna make it stop, baby. I'll take the pain away." I plastered my lips to hers, and as soon as I made contact, she stopped shaking and stilled beneath me. I pulled back so I could see if the mist stopped moving, but instead it was making its way up her body faster now. I turned to the others to see if they knew what to do and how to stop it. None of them were looking at me—they were all focusing on Ryan.

"Dominic, you, Alex, and Chase are going to need to hold that force field tight. Nico, move away from her, everyone needs to move back near the chapel doors now."

I turned to my sister, who had a serious look on her face. I don't know why, but in this moment I trusted my sister's advice, and we all moved to the back of the church and huddled in close. "Mya, I need you to help me make a barrier around us. When she expels that power, we are gonna need a shield. Nico can't help us; his power is locked in with Ryan's."

I was staring at my sister in awe. How did she know all of this? Mya and Sophia didn't waste any time. They both quickly started chanting, and a yellow and purple barrier started to shimmer in front of us. My sister wasn't a weak witch anymore; she was strong and powerful, a force to be reckoned with. My attention was pulled back toward Ryan when she let out a gut-wrenching scream. I really hope these force fields the guys had up would mute the sounds from traveling outside.

We all watched, transfixed on the sight before us. Ryan was completely covered in blue mist now. It was like a cocoon wrapped around her. Her groaning and screaming stopped. We all waited with bated breath to see what would happen next. Is it over? Is she okay? I looked to the others, seeking out their thoughts, when I heard someone gasp. I turned back toward where Ryan was and saw the mist had lifted her into the air. She was floating, arms stretched out wide, her dress rippling like it was blowing in the breeze. There was no wind in the chapel.

CHAPTER 41
Ryan

I felt weightless and free, like a missing piece from inside me had been finally put back. I was whole for the first time in my life. My worries and fears weren't so troubling anymore. I felt like I was strong enough to take on the world. I didn't want to open my eyes and ruin this moment or the feelings I had; I knew I couldn't keep my head buried in the sand forever.

I reluctantly peeled my eyes open and frowned in confusion. I could see Nico, Jax, Kai, Dom, Alex, Chase, Mya, Aurora, and Sophia all standing at the back of the chapel. There was a bubble around them that was shimmering yellow and purple.

Why were they behind the bubble? I looked around to see all the walls shimmering as well; it reminded me of the dome I had made the other day. Why were they looking up at me?

I looked down, and that's when I noticed, I was floating mid fucking air with a blue mist surrounding me!

What the actual fuck is going on? I started to panic. I could see Nico's mouth moving, but I couldn't hear what he was saying from this side of the dome. What's happening to me?

Why couldn't I get back down to the ground? I felt heat creeping its way up my body, making me panic more, thinking I was going to start burning from the inside again.

I looked to the others, asking them to help me. Jax and Kai were holding Nico back. I was really starting to freak out when the heat intensified and worked its way down my arms. I stretched my arms open wider, and instead of fighting the burning sensation, this time I chose to embrace it.

I leaned my head back and let out a shriek from deep within. It wasn't from the magic, but me letting go of all the pain I had suffered in my life. I felt pressure build in my chest, and that's when it happened—a force so strong it burst out of me, and all I could see was blue light. The more I was pushing whatever this was inside me out, the more I felt free and less constricted.

It was so freeing to release all this pent-up energy from inside me. I felt more in control now. As the pressure inside me lessened, I felt myself slowly float back down to the ground. As soon as my feet hit the ground, I dropped to my knees, exhaustion suddenly taking over my body. The chapel was ruined.

The pews were a splintered mess on the ground, and the windows were smashed. The flowers were burned to a crisp, and even the chandelier was broken.

I leaned over, placing my hands on the ground in front of me so I could try to stabilize myself. I was panting hard, trying to catch my breath. After a couple of minutes, I saw someone kneel down in front of me and then two hands were placed on my shoulders. My head felt so heavy I could barely lift it, but I pushed through and lifted my head to see who was in front of me. Two violet eyes stared back at me, concern evident on his face.

"Are you okay, love?" Nico moved his hands from my shoulders to cup my cheeks, and his touch was like a balm warding off the heat inside me. At his touch I started to feel relaxed and content. My body felt like it was being pulled toward him, and a voice inside my head was telling me he could make it all better. Call me crazy, but I believed that voice. Nico didn't waste another second. He scooped me up and cradled me in his lap, stroking the hair out of my face. "You're okay, baby, I've got you." I couldn't get my voice to work, so I nodded instead. Looking around, I could see the others had formed a circle around us, displaying varying looks of awe, shock, concern, and worry. I didn't have the energy to try and decipher those looks. Mya and Sophia looked like they were ready to pass out. The most concerning thing for me right now though is why Dom, Alex and Chase looked like they had seen a ghost. What the fuck happened?

"Are you okay, Ry?" I gave Aurora a smile and nodded my head. Truth was, I felt like I could sleep for days.

"Soph, are you okay?"

"I feel like I am going to pass out, brother, I don't know how Mya and I managed to hold that shield against that blast."

"I agree, I am wiped out. I have never in my life stood against a force as strong as that. I am very grateful Sophia and I were able to hold the shield, or we would all be dead right now." I cuddled deeper into Nico at Mya's foreboding tone. I felt free in that moment, and alive, while my friends and *husband* were fighting for their lives against my power. Nico was rubbing my back and holding me tighter, trying his best to comfort me.

"The true heroes are you three guys; you've done amazing holding the blast. You guys saved a lot of lives here today." I turned my head to see Dom and my cousins with their heads down. Chase started shaking his head from side to side. Why are they so down? They had done so well. I owe them so much for what they had done. I owe all of these guys so much.

"We didn't, Jackson...we tried, but..." Dom cut in and spoke for Chase, looking at me and making eye contact for the first time.

"We couldn't hold the blast, love. I'm sorry."

Speaking for the first time since the incident, I asked, "What do you mean, Dom? What happened?" Dom dropped his gaze, and I felt Nico tense beneath me. I looked to both my cousins for reassurance, but both their heads were still hanging down.

"Answer her, Dom! What happened?" Nico was trying hard to contain his frustration. Dom opened and shut his mouth a few times but said nothing, and a pit of dread was starting to form in my stomach. Then out of nowhere, Jax dropped to his knees and started gripping his hair with both hands.

"No, no, no—we did everything right! How the fuck did this happen?" I saw tears rolling down Jackson's face, and he seemed like he was in pain.

"Dominic, what the fuck happened?" Sophia shouted. Dom wouldn't make eye contact with anyone. Alex spoke, and fuck my life—I really wish Alex let me live in my naïve bubble for a bit longer, because what he had to say changed everything. I was royally fucked, and I deserved everything coming my way for what I had just done.

"We couldn't hold the force field. The reason why yours and Mya's shield held was because Dom, Chase, and I helped you hold it. In doing so, the force field weakened, and Ryan shattered it to smithereens. We fucked up, and they all paid the price." Alex had tears leaking from his eyes.

"How many, Jackson?" I looked to Kai then, who was waiting for Jackson's answer.

"At least fifty." Oh my God, I killed fifty people! I'm a murderer. I am no better than my sister. I'm a killer.

"We need to run now! I have to take her to Farrarie, where they can't get her. I'll convince the elders it was an accident."

Why did Nico want to hide me? Who was going to take me? Everyone started talking at once, trying to make a plan, while I sat there cradled in Nico's lap with silent tears rolling down my face.

I deserved everything that was coming my way. Everyone stopped talking as soon as the chapel doors banged open. Nico stood with me cradled in his arms and turned to face the doorway.

Kai, Jax, and Dom moved to stand in front of us to block me from the view of whoever entered. Alex and Chase moved to stand in front of Mya, Aurora, and Sophia. Their tense posture put me on edge, and I strained my neck to see around the guys so I could see who entered and put everyone on guard, but they were too bloody big and wide, and I couldn't see around them, even with the added height of being in Nico's arms.

"Alpha, as this is your land, we are asking you to step aside quietly. This does not need to get out of hand; we just need the girl."

"She will be returning to Farrarie with me, Lachlan; there is no need for your presence here." Nico's voice held so much authority that even I would have obeyed him. Whoever this man was, Nico sure as shit didn't like him. His arms tightened around me, securing me closer to his chest.

"She will remain here in the custody of the vampires. She is your wife, so she cannot return to the fae realm." I was really starting to get scared now; this Lachlan guy wasn't backing down. What was going to happen to me?

"Then she will remain here with me and my pack."

"She will not. You are too close to the accused and her husband; therefore she will be remanded into the care of the vampire king." What the fuck! I am not going anywhere with Randall fucking Cane.

"Fuck that. She can be held at the Knox coven until her

hearing." What the hell, Chase? Stevie would kill me if I went there.

"No, Mr. Knox, she will not return to her coven. I am tired of this conversation. Hand the girl over or we will take her from you!" I looked up at Nico, trying to convey to him with my eyes that I didn't want to go, I wanted to stay with him.

CHAPTER 42

Looking down at her, I can see the fear in her eyes, and I would rather die than hand her over to those fucking leeches. I look around the chapel, trying to find a way to escape. I've been trying to access my magic since I learned the guys didn't contain the blast. I don't know what the hell is going on. If I can't access my magic, I can't even open a portal. Where the fuck are Maverick and Larick? I saw them here earlier, and they should be here right now, helping there fucking queen.

I can see Dom's lips moving, and I start to hope. My brother is opening me a portal to run and take Ryan away from here. I'll deal with my magic problem later. Dom's lips start moving faster. What the fuck is taking him so long?

"Are you going to do this the hard way or the easy way?" No one says anything. Lachlan sighs and shakes his head. "I figured it would be the hard way, pity." Lachlan calls out to whomever to come in, and when I see who they are, I know we are fucked.

I have to find a way out of this. I am the king of the fucking fae and married to the most powerful supernatural on the planet, so why can't I access my fucking magic?

"Dad?" I follow Chase's line of sight toward the Knox coven elders and see a tall muscular man with black hair and blue eyes. The man cuts his gaze to Chase and then Alex, and a private conversation must transpire between them, because Alex starts nodding. The Knox coven elders are here in the chapel—all of them.

"Bring the girl to me or the elders will take her from you." Fuck, I lean forward slightly to whisper in Kai's ear. I need more time to think of a plan.

"We will bring her outside." Ryan turns to stone in my arms at Kai's words. Lachlan nods and turns to exit the chapel with the elders following him. "Make a fucking portal and leave now!" Kai whisper-shouts at me as we slowly walk toward the exit.

"I can't. I don't know what's happening, but I have no access to my magic." At my admission, Ryan starts to tremble in my arms. Fuck, she's scared, and I can't even protect her right now.

"I can't access mine either. I tried to before, because you were taking too long." That's why Dom was chanting faster; he was getting pissed, his magic was muted for some reason. As we were nearing the end of the aisle, Chase spoke.

"No one can access their magic right now, not even Ryan."

"What are you talking about?" Dom took the words right out of my mouth. We all stopped and stared, waiting for him to answer. "My dad and the other elders are wearing the moon stones around their necks. I don't know how they found them or where they got them from, they were supposed to be a myth or a legend."

"What is a fucking moon stone, boy?" Shit, Kai was at the end of his patience now.

"The moon stone can mute all magic. It can stop the cravings of a vampire and stop a wolf from shifting. They are the most powerful stones, and they are supposed to have been destroyed centuries ago." How the fuck did Mya know about this and I didn't?

"Hurry up, boy." I tensed at the sound of Randall's voice. He was outside waiting with the elders, fuck. Looking around our group, and seeing everyone here prepared to fight with nothing but our fists, to save my wife, meant so much to me. Each one of them gave me a nod, telling me that whatever I decide to do, they are with me. We reluctantly and cautiously exit the chapel and descend the stairs. Standing in front of us is none other than Randall fucking Cane. On either side of him is the elder council from the vampires, led by Lachlan, and then on the other side is the Knox coven elders.

"I can't access my pack through our mind link."

"You can't use your link or magic of any kind, Jax; the moon stone prevents it." Fuck, Mya was just full of good news tonight, wasn't she?

"Hand her over, boy, and I promise I'll take *real* good care of her." I'll snap that slimy cunt's neck the next chance I get.

Looking down at Ryan, seeing her eyes so vacant, nearly broke me. She has been through so much and pushed her emotions down so far to help me and my people. After what happened tonight and the deaths of so many on her hands, she couldn't lock away her emotions any longer. I leaned down and kissed her lips and then whispered in her ear.

"I love you, Ryan, and I will fight for you always, my love. When this is over, little one, I will help you get through the guilt of tonight, and I will help you get vengeance for your father as well." I moved toward Dominic and placed Ryan in his arms; he looked shocked, but what he must see on my face snaps him out of it, and he quickly cradles her to his chest. I lean in to whisper in his ear. "If this doesn't work, you take her and you run. I will buy you as much time as I can, but you run and you take her home as soon as you have access to your magic." I pull back and look Dom in the eye.

"You have my word, brother." Turning around I face the elders and Randall.

"What transpired here tonight was an accident; we were unaware that our union would be the key to unlocking my wife's fae magic." I heard a couple of the elders gasp. I was lying through my teeth, and then I noticed that wolves and witches were starting to gather around. I hope they were on our side and not against us. "My wife never meant to hurt anyone."

"But she did, so hand her over now!"

"Fuck you, Randall. You killed Jackson's father and you are trying to seal my realm so my world will die. You should be the one standing trial." I can hear the wolves and witches around us gasp. The Knox elders and vampire elders don't seem shocked. Why isn't Lachlan shocked, did he know?

"You are a liar and have no proof, boy. I am not the one who has locked the *true* queen of the Knox coven in a cell." At Randall's outburst, Lachlan turns his gaze to me.

"Is this true, Nico? Have you got Stevie Knox locked in a cell?" Fuck, I want to slap that sly smirk off Randall's fucking face. Where the fuck are the fae elders? I nod my head.

"Release her now!"

"You can't release her, she is dangerous."

"The only dangerous person here is the woman you all are so intent on protecting! Now release her." Jax turns around, looking for someone, and then proceeds to tell them they have to find one of the two guards who can access the cells and bring Stevie to us. We wait until Luther, Jackson's guard, comes back with Stevie. She is smiling from ear to ear and almost skipping. That bitch is crazy.

"Miss Knox, I wasn't aware that you were held captive."

"Since when do elders get involved in shit like this, Lachlan?"

"Since two leaders have died so close together and both of them have the scent of fae on them, that's when, Dominic!" I winced at his outburst. Lachlan was angry, and he was also a very fucking powerful vamp. I don't blame him, but he had it wrong. It wasn't us, it was Randall and Stevie, and we needed to prove it. "Hand the girl over, Nico." Yeah, that's not gonna happen.

"The girl can remain here in the custody of the shifter elders." I turn my head to see Mr. Silver limping toward us; he's leaning heavily on a cane, trying to hold himself up. I turn my gaze to Dom, who is shocked and then that look turns to anger. His father can't use his shifter healing because of the moon stones.

"Ian, a pleasure to see you, old friend."

"And you, Lachlan."

"The girl cannot remain here, Ian. she is too close to the alpha. She must be held by the vampire elders, as we are the only neutral clan."

"Randall has her mother imprisoned and is actively trying to kill her, and so is that fucking psycho coven queen."

"You have no proof, my dear Sophia." Sophia starts to tremble at the way Randall is speaking to her.

"I have had enough!" Stevie shouts, and then I'm sailing through the air and hitting the front of the chapel, I look around to see that the rest of our group has been thrown against the chapel, as well. Aurora seems to be hurt badly, as she's not moving. Jackson starts growling, but there is nothing he can do. We have no magic. We all dropped to the ground, but still held there by magic. How the fuck can Stevie use magic and we can't? I'm struggling and fighting as hard as I can. I have never been subdued by anyone else's magic before, except for Dom. Something is seriously wrong with Stevie; if she had that much power, she could have broken out of those cells easily. I can feel the power radiating off her, she feels as strong as Ryan.

She starts walking toward Dominic with a huge smile on her face.

"Stop right there and stay away from my son!" Stevie turns toward Mr. Silver and smiles, with a flick of her wrist, Mr. Silver is sent flying. Dom immediately starts to shake, torn between going to his father and protecting Ryan.

"Ooops, I hope your daddy is going to be okay." The crazy bitch laughs, and everyone around the clearing is standing there in shock., I notice now a few of my people are gathering, and some vampires are here now too. The witches look terrified, and the shifters are torn, wanting to attack and protect their alpha but waiting for his orders. The vampires are bloodthirsty and want to fight, disgusting fucking leeches. Scanning the clearing, I spot Maverick. He sees me looking at him and I shake my head, telling him with my eyes to hold off on an attack. We're far too outnumbered.

"You're a crazy fucking bitch, you know that? You will never win. Ryan is ten times the woman you will ever be. Enjoy your reign while it lasts, because your sister is coming for *her* throne." Stevie slaps Dom clean across the cheek, making his head snap to the side. Sophia starts going nuts, fighting against the magic holding her in place.

"I'll fucking kill you! Stay the fuck away from him, you evil bitch!" Stevie ignores Sophia's outburst.

"Hand her over now, or I start hurting your friends. Starting with the mouthy fucking fae bitch." No! not my sister! Dom turns to look at Sophia and then back to me. I can see he's torn, and fuck, so am I. I can't lose my sister again, but I can't lose Ryan either.

"Take me instead!" I shout.

"Aww that's so cute, but no." Stevie raises here hand and Sophia starts to float toward her. As soon as Soph is within her grasp, Stevie grips her by the throat and starts to choke her.

"Lachlan, do something!" The fucking bastard stands there watching on in horror at what he is seeing. He needs to stop this. Everyone is frozen in place except for the vamps and witches. We underestimated Stevie, and now my sister will pay the price. Soph is struggling to breathe.

"Stop! I'll do whatever you want. I'll seal the fucking fae realm if I have to!" I hear gasps all around at Dom's outburst; Soph is starting to turn purple. "Let her go and I'll seal it, I swear."

"Enough!" Stevie releases my sister, who drops to the ground, gasping for air and clawing at her throat. Ryan wiggles out of Dom's arms to stand on her feet, and Dom rushes to Soph and picks her up, moving back toward the chapel stairs near the rest of us.

"I was having fun, Ry. You're a party pooper." Stevie's eyes are pitch black, you can see black liquid swimming beneath her skin. I can see Ryan is shaky on her legs and trembling. She exerted so much power tonight that she is weak. "Come with us now and none of them will be harmed. If you delay any longer and try something stupid, I will do something like this." She clicks her fingers and then I hear Aurora scream. Looking over at her, I see it now, blood is dripping down the front of her head. She must have hit her head hard against the chapel wall, and on top of that, Stevie just broke her arm. "Or this." Now Chase is screaming out; Stevie broke his leg, and it's hanging at an odd angle. His father steps forward for the first time tonight, but pauses when he sees Stevie is looking at him. "Or..."

"Stop! You have my word I will come with you without a fight." Ryan turns to look back at me. I'm stuck on the ground fighting against my restraints like a worthless dog while my wife is standing in front of a deranged killer. Ryan smiles a broken smile and mouths *come for me*. I see the tears in her eyes and the doubt, but I will never stop until I find her. I harden my facial features and nod. I'll come for you, baby, and I'll kill everyone in my fucking way.

Epilogue

RYAN

I've been sitting in a cell for nearly two weeks, beaten and barely lucid. I am injected with something three times a day. I don't know what's in the injection; not five minutes after they inject me, I black out. Randall comes to me every day and withdraws blood from me. I don't know what he needs the blood for, and I would have thought he would have killed me by now. Every time the darkness takes over, I try to reach my dreamland with Nico. I have even tried to reach Kai, but nothing happens. I held out hope for the first few days that Nico and the guys would come for me, but they have left me here. I knew it was too good to be true.

"Are you awake?" I turn my head slowly; it's such an effort to move even my head. Every bone in my body is aching and sore. I am beaten three times a day, after every injection; they beat me before I pass out. "I heard the guards talking. There is a big elder meeting. All four of the elder councils are coming here today."

"What..." Clearing my dry throat, I try to speak again. "What does that mean?"

"Something big is going down." I wasn't holding out hope. If

Nico was coming for me, he would have already been here. I felt used. He married me and then left me. Well, I left him, really, but I did it to save their lives. Stevie enjoyed hearing Nico scream out for me as she dragged me by my hair all the way to the car the night of my wedding. Randall has tried to get me to use my powers when I'm brought to him in his office, but for some reason I can't use them. Normally all it took was for me to be angry and then I would blast shit, but now, I can't even do that.

"I think they're coming for you."

"Trust me, no one is coming for me. My husband left me here to rot, my cousins haven't come, and my friends haven't shown up either. They all probably think I'm dead and are celebrating that the fae realm can live on." I could hear the bitterness and heartbreak in my own voice, but I wouldn't shed another tear for what I had lost.

"Don't say that, Smurfy." I hated the nickname as soon as he had come up with it; I told him I glowed blue when I used magic, and ever since he had been calling me Smurfy. We can't actually see each other, as it's pitch black in the cells. We have no lights down here at all.

"If I ever get to blow this joint, I promise I won't leave without you."

"Yes, you will. Everyone leaves me."

"Not me, Smurfy, I got your back all day. I swear." The stupidest and weirdest part is I believed him.

Changing the subject, I ask my jail buddy, "You still haven't told me why you're in here?"

"My mom was a prisoner here for many years and died, apparently. The king told me I had to live out the rest of her sentence. I was born here, so I know no other life. For nearly seventeen years, this is all I have known."

"I swear to you, if *I* ever blow this joint, I will not leave without you, Lucian."

Click the link below to continue reading book 3
A Beautiful Nightmare

Secret Society/ Bully

Filthy Few

Forever Filthy

Filthiest Of Them All

Masked Men Novella (Pure Smut)

Dirty Priest

Dirty Daddy

Sports Romance

Playing For Keeps

Offside

Touchdown

End Game

Hail Mary

Blindside

RH Sports

Hate Us Like You Mean It

MM

Love Me Like You Mean It

Paranormal Romance

The Veil Of Obsidian

Of Time And Carnage

Curse Of Fate

Dream

Fate

Nightmare

Redemption

Anarchy

<u>Brutal Savages</u>

Savage Lies

Brutal Truth

Savage Beast

Brutal Beauty

Acknowledgments

First and foremost, thank you to my babies for being so amazing and helping me with my tiktoks, you two are my world. I love you forever and always!

My girls,
Sammy, Kim and Fee.
Where do I even begin?
You three are my go to and my support team.
Sammy thank you for everything you have done to help me get these books where they needed to be.
Kat, thank you for all the love and support and being there for me.
Fee, my girl, thank you for always being my sound board and allowing me to vent whenever I needed to.
I love you ladies dearly. xxx

A huge THANK YOU to Kelsey Clayton, woman you are fucking awesome! Without you none of this would be possible. You have taken me under your wing and helped guide me, I cannot thank you enough K.C. xxx

About the Author

Samantha Barrett is originally from Auckland, New Zealand but living in Brisbane, Australia.

Sam writes all things dirty dark and delicious with a side of twisted mind fuck.

She is a lover of all things red flags and an anti-hero is a must.